The Girl Who Applied Everywhere

John J. Binder

To my children, John, Kevin, and Kristin, who have all survived the college search process.

Advance Praise for *The Girl Who Applied Everywhere*

"It's *Do Black Patent Leather Shoes Really Reflect Up?* meets *Confederacy of Dunces*–with some *Sixteen Candles, Animal House,* and even Three Stooges thrown in for good measure. Which equals a ton of laughs. Ultimately though the ridiculous accentuates the positive because there's a moral or two here for not only the college applicants but also their overzealous parents and the people in university admissions." – Tim Weithers, Associate Director, Graduate Program in Financial Mathematics, University of Chicago.

"This is a delightful read for anyone who has ever dealt with college admissions . . . such as students, parents, counselors, teachers, and college officials. Imaginative writing is reflected in a not so far-fetched humorous story that many of us could easily identify with as we watched our own kids make college decisions. Subtle twists and turns in the thinking of three teenagers keeps the satirical plot unfolding until the unexpected conclusion." – Emanuel D. Pollack, Senior Associate Dean, College of Liberal Arts and Sciences, University of Illinois at Chicago.

"John Binder has captured the essence of the college admissions process, from an entirely different angle, and consequently this book is interesting as well as informative. The author uses his experience as both a father, who watched his children apply to college, and as a university administrator, who ran a graduate program including the admissions office, to carefully explore a complicated subject. There are important points to ponder here, even if you don't agree with all of them, for anyone who has ever been involved with college applications and admissions, including the overwrought parents of the applicants.

Some students get bogged down trying to begin their college application procedure, others in selecting the right schools and completing the applications. Institutions get bogged down in various phases of the review, acceptance, and admissions decision making. No one will get bogged down reading this book – although you might laugh so hard that you will hurt yourself." – Walter H. Washington, Associate Dean of Undergraduate Programs (retired), College of Business Administration, University of Illinois at Chicago.

"Entertaining and thought provoking." – Jessica Young, History teacher, Oak Park-River Forest High School.

"An interesting glance at the contemporary high school experience." – Brendan Lee, English teacher, Oak Park-River Forest High School.

Praise for *The Chicago Outfit*

"Brilliant! The Chicago Outfit by John Binder tells it all! If you're interested in the history of organized crime in the streets and businesses of Chicago from the 19th century to the present . . . this is it!" – Tony Stewart, author, *Dillinger, The Hidden Truth.*

"John Binder's The Chicago Outfit is a must-have for any serious researcher's library. The pictures and commentary bring an era and its criminals to life like no other work has done." – Rose Keefe, author, *Guns and Roses: The Untold Story of Dean O'Banion.*

CONTENTS

ACKNOWLEDGMENTS

Many thanks to Diane Dygert, Jeff Gusfield, Brendan Lee, Chrys Meador, Steve Skapek, Walter Washington, Tim Weithers, and Jessica Young, who read the manuscript and freely shared their comments, criticisms, and suggestions with me. I also owe much to Bill Brashler, Rose Keefe, and Allen Salter (aka Sam Reaves), all fine authors, who have provided me with valuable advice about writing and publishing over the years.

Finally, I am especially indebted to Phil Loveall, a man of great wit and skill. Besides reviewing an early draft of the manuscript in detail, once upon a time he taught a young sophomore at Maine East High School how to write.

1
THE BEGINNING

"Where are you going to college?"

It seemed that Sarah Jennings had been answering that question most of her life. When she first heard of college–at least the first time she remembered hearing about it–Sarah was a second grader sitting with her family in Oak Stream, just west of Chicago. An old community, with oak trees in abundance and a small river running through it, Oak Stream is on one of the commuter rail lines that connect the outlying areas to the city. Once very conservative and lily-white, it is now fairly progressive as Chicago suburbs go, although in a funny sort of way, and quite eclectic. Oak Stream has not only a large African American population but also a gay community, giving it a diversity many of the western suburbs lacked. You might go so far as to say that over time it had become a village of narrow lawns and broad minds.

At the time Sarah's brother Ben was in fourth grade and her younger brother, Kevin, was four. Ben was fully aware that there was something in the educational system beyond high school and that smart kids, a group he belonged to, went there. He brought the subject up one night at the dinner table.

"Dad, where did you go to college?"

"I went to Brown. It's in Rhode Island," John Jennings said from the head of the table. A successful business executive, he looked the part with an intelligent face and searching eyes. He had loosened the tie around his neck as soon as he had come home, and his suit jacket hung on the chair behind him

"Is that where you met Mom?"

"No, we met here in Chicago. Dad came back home after college, and

1

I moved here to take a job," Kate Jennings, a blonde and very young looking thirty-five-year-old with a quick mind, answered. She was proud of her bright children.

"Then where did you go?"

"I went to Notre Dame."

"The place in South Bend with the famous football team?"

"Yes, Ben, right by your grandparents."

"Sarah, where are you going to go to college?" little Kevin asked innocently.

"I'm going to go to Notre Dame like Mommy," she chirped with a huge smile. It was important to Sarah that people liked her, and by going to Notre Dame she felt she would win her parents' approval.

"You don't go to a college because Mom went there. You go there to learn things," Ben said firmly.

"Oh," Sarah replied sheepishly.

Over the next ten years she was asked the same question innumerable times and received advice from virtually everyone who asked her, whether she wanted it or not. It eventually made her head spin.

This is the story of how her head spun.

2
THE HISTORY KIDS

In high school, Rob Taylor and Carrie Wilson were Sarah's best friends. They walked to school together, ate lunch together, and spent most of their free time together. There had been a few dates for Sarah and Carrie starting in the eighth grade, but the boys found them a bit overwhelming and largely stayed away. Rob's off-the-wall sense of humor was the best girl repellant known to man, and Sarah's wit did nothing to help her with the boys either. Although the outside world did not always understand them, they understood each other and appreciated the bond they had forged.

Sarah had known Rob since second grade in Mrs. Reinhart's class. Helga Reinhart was from the old school and resented having students who were too far removed from the average in either direction. That created extra work for her. Because Rob and Sarah were the two brightest kids in the class, she seated them together. She also put them out in the hall or in the library with workbooks containing advanced topics whenever she felt that class material was not challenging enough for them. Having been thus joined together, the elementary schools did not tear them asunder in their remaining years. When they reached high school, Rob, who was short for a boy his age, stood two inches below Sarah's height. Perennially clad in jeans and a T-shirt, his hair and the glasses he wore gave him a disheveled resemblance to Harry Potter. At fourteen, Sarah wore her blonde hair fairly short, as she would throughout high school. The hair style complemented her physique and green eyes. Like Rob, she favored simple clothing, but unlike him it suited her.

They met Carrie on their first day at Oak Stream High School in Honors American history. Carrie was of average height, with pretty, shoulder-length brown hair that had a touch of red in it. Round glasses

3

concealed her probing eyes. As the lanky and lethargic Mr. Harrison droned on, naming names and writing dates on the blackboard, Carrie, who sat in front of Sarah and next to Rob, muttered under her breath, "This is going to be a long year."

"Hey, my brother had this guy two years ago. The tests are all names and dates, so you have to memorize those to get an A," Sarah whispered. "But the good news is that the textbook is great, and the library actually has a ton of interesting books on American history."

"Thanks for that," Carrie replied.

In the hallway after class they made the usual introductions and agreed to talk among themselves about history, which led to many shared books, weekend study sessions, long discussions of "Why?" and "What If?" and edits of each other's papers. Early in their freshman year they were already such fast friends that Rob observed, "We spend as much time together as the Three Musketeers."

It was Sarah's favorite book. She responded, "Then we need a motto. How about 'One for All and All for One'?"

"Perfect," Carrie remarked.

Whenever possible, they were on the same team for class projects, which did not always endear them to the other students.

The one truly interesting thing about Mr. Harrison's class—which had students guessing each year who he stole the idea from—was the project on the colonization of North America. After the usual discussion of the various Georges and Louies who were kings at the time, Mr. Harrison had the students form three-person teams. Each team represented a fictitious European country, whose name had to end in "ia," that colonized part of the continental United States in 1750. The students determined all the defining features of the colony and were limited only by basic historical facts. At the end of the module they had to turn in a written report followed by a presentation in class. If there was any overlap in the lands claimed, wars resulted and Mr. Harrison determined the winners and the ownership of lands in the New World afterward.

The plans of most of the teams were common knowledge. Many of them claimed territory along the Mississippi, Ohio, and/or Missouri Rivers, which was perhaps not surprising for kids from the Midwest, and fashioned small, simple colonies with between 25,000 and 50,000 settlers. Carrie, Rob, and Sarah had other ideas. They met one weekend at Rob's house to work out the details.

"All right, guys, so we're taking the entire center of the map--all the lands along the Mississippi River and its tributaries."

"Yup, that's the idea, Sarah. But now we have to hold onto it. It sounds like at least seven other teams are colonizing part of this area," Carrie stated.

"That's what I heard," Rob offered. "Otherwise, Britannia is on the eastern seaboard, essentially the area of the thirteen original British colonies. Espania is taking land in the West, approximately California, Arizona, and Nevada. Lusitania has part of what is New England, something like the current state of Maine."

"Francia is claiming the lower quarter of the Mississippi River Valley, down to the Gulf of Mexico. But we don't have to worry about them. I know Kathy Bates on that team, and the only thing she cares about is going to the mall. Not surprisingly, her group does not like the wilderness and will sell us their claims in the New World."

"They didn't ask for a discount at Macy's?" Rob asked Sarah. "Great, we have a lock on the mouth of the river."

"I suggest we have 500,000 settlers in total. We're going to have to be big to support a good-sized army."

"Agreed," both Rob and Sarah chimed in.

"In terms of the military, we have good relations with our mother country. They have, say, 25,000 regular troops stationed in the colony. Twenty regiments of infantry and five of cavalry, at 1,000 men per regiment, and each infantry regiment has ten cannon. That's separate from artillery in our forts and the fortifications in our major cities. Is that OK?"

Carrie and Rob nodded.

"We'll organize the colonists into militia units which can be called up for six months of service by the Crown, extendable in case of an emergency. They're all crack shots and well trained in New World forest tactics. How about a militia of 75,000 men in total?"

"Ah, Rob, that sounds maybe a little high. Didn't the families have lots of children back then?" Carrie answered, biting off a fingernail on her left hand.

"Well, they had lots of kids, but boys roughly sixteen years old were considered men and very old men were also available for military service. Although I get your point. Let me check the earliest census to see if we can get a handle on this."

Rob retreated a few feet to his computer and googled the U.S. Census.

"In the 1790 about a quarter of the free white population in the United States consisted of males 16 and over. That would be 125,000 adult males in our total population. Not all of them would be in the militia though. If we use half that number, that's over 60,000. OK, how about a militia of 50,000 men expandable in emergencies to 60,000?"

"Fine. What about the Indian tribes in our area?"

"They're called Native Americans," Rob responded dryly. He was one-eighth Potawatomi; both his father's paternal grandparents were one-half Potawatomi. Rob's father was interested in his heritage and frequently took the family to visit the tribe's lands in Wisconsin to learn about their culture.

"My bad. What about the Native Americans?" Carrie asked after rewording the question.

"I've been thinking about that. We will have an alliance with all the tribes in the area we claim."

"Good one, Rob," Sarah interjected .

"Hey, wait. I'm not done yet. We also have a treaty with all the tribes in the areas neighboring our colony. Same terms. That should give us roughly half as many warriors as militia from inside the colony and another 10,000 warriors or so from the surrounding areas, which really sticks it to our enemies."

"Great, that comes to 25,000 regular troops, 50,000 to 60,000 militia, and about 35,000 Native American warriors," Carrie concluded. "We can also make treaties with Britannia, Espania, and Lusitania—and their colonies if they've separated off—to create an alliance in the New World. I think we should also create a European alliance including Francia as a partner because they're out of the New World now."

Carrie bit off another fingernail, causing Sarah to say, "You're almost out of nails, Carrie."

"Sorry. I can't help it," she pleaded.

Finished with the military, they moved on to other details of their colony.

A few weeks later the written reports were turned in, and it was time for the presentations. After reading the student reports, Mr. Harrison assigned Sarah, Rob, and Carrie to go last.

The other teams created colonies that were as expected, based on the gossip about what everyone was doing. Almost all of them were independent from their mother countries and were completely agricultural. The presentations by the other groups lacked real detail, and Mr. Harrison appeared terminally bored as he listened.

Carrie did the talking for their team.

"Hi. Rob, Sarah, and I represent the nation of Dementia, which is a major European power. Our colony in the New World is called Dementia Minor." The name was Rob's idea.

The joke flew over the heads of most of the students, but Mr. Harrison burst out laughing. He put his hand in front of his face to conceal his amusement.

"Dementia Minor is essentially a democracy, in which the colonists elect representatives to the assembly in the capital. The assembly's votes are advisory to the parliament and king of Dementia, but on most matters they follow the colonists' wishes. The mother country taxes Dementia Minor to pay for the military support it provides, but otherwise the colony is economically independent. The population of Dementia Minor is 500,000."

"That's way too large," someone muttered in the back of the room.

"Our colony has capitalism as its economic system and has free trade with the mother country, as well as all other countries and their colonies. It has thriving agriculture, natural resources in the form of timber, furs and minerals, and also manufacturing. These factories produce many of the goods consumed in the colony, including most of the muskets and gunpowder. Swords and cannon are primarily imported from Dementia but there are numerous iron works in the colony. Native Americans in Dementia Minor can only trade with the Dementia Trading Company."

Carrie turned next to the military aspects of Dementia Minor and its diplomatic relations. She outlined the army and the colony's alliances before continuing.

"Our city of New Orleans, part of the claim we have purchased from Francia, is heavily fortified and defended by regular troops from Dementia and colonial militia, supported by heavy artillery. In the event of war, we will close the Mississippi River to our enemies. Dementia has a fleet of 30 ships of the line, supported by frigates, stationed in the Gulf of Mexico to enforce any war time blockade. We also have forts at various points along the river, such as where the Ohio and Missouri flow into it, to block shipments by our enemies."

The other teams had not considered any of these points. Facial expressions changed for the worse as a few students recognized their importance.

"To conclude our presentation, Dementia Minor claims all the land drained by the Mississippi River and its tributaries, including the Ohio and the Missouri rivers."

"Thank you, Carrie. Tomorrow I'll present the final map of the New World, after the Treaty of Geneva has been signed by the combatants."

Even though the project did not count heavily toward their course grade, there was a sense of anticipation in Honors history the next morning. Before Mr. Harrison could step to the board, the very large Tim Tyler, one of the three football players representing Hibernia, raised his hand.

Tyler was so strong that some kids whispered he was using steroids. Rob had bumped into him in the bathroom the first day of school before classes started. As he was washing his hands, Tim and some guys on the football team came through the door. Looking down at Rob, Tim Tyler joked, "Hey, you're pretty short. Are you sure you're a freshman?"

His friends burst out laughing. Playing to the audience, Tyler pointed toward central Oak Stream as he strode up to the urinals and remarked, "Sixth grade is that way."

As he was leaving the bathroom, Rob turned and responded, while pointing in another direction. "You're pretty big. Can you actually read and write? First grade is that way."

To Rob's surprise, later that morning he found Tim Tyler glaring at him from a few feet away in Honors American history.

"Yes, Tim?" Mr. Harrison asked, acknowledging his hand.

"Mr. Harrison, New Hibernia has entered into a treaty to fight Dementia Minor . . ."

"Mr. Tyler, all colonial features must appear in the written reports turned in before the presentations."

"But they knew what we were going to do."

"Only because you talked about it. Discretion is a valuable asset in a statesman, Mr. Tyler."

When Rob smirked, Tim Tyler caught Rob's expression out of the corner of his eye. In a low tone he said, "Bet you worked on this twenty-four hours a day, you little jerkoff. Get a life."

"Hey, Tim, are you familiar with the song 'If I Only Had a Brain' from the *Wizard of Oz*?" Rob responded.

"Kiss my ass."

"Pull your head out, and I will."

A look from the teacher quieted them. Mr. Harrison hung a large map of the United States from clips at the top of the blackboard. It was blank except for the major rivers and mountain ranges.

"Based on the written reports and the resulting wars, which have been settled by the Treaty of Geneva in late 1750, this is what the New World looks like. New Britannia is here on the East Coast," he said, outlining an area with blue marker. Changing colors, he continued. "New Lusitania is in the Northeast and New Espania is on the West Coast. Your mother countries were the only ones to claim these areas, so there were no wars for control of them."

"Francia sold its claims in the New World to Dementia, and presumably the colonists have returned to Paris to go shopping," he said in the direction of Kathy Bates. "This leaves the countries claiming land in the area drained by the Mississippi River and its tributaries." Mr. Harrison looked at the students, taking an orange marker from his desk. "New Irlandia retains what is roughly western Colorado. All the rest of this area is now part of Dementia Minor, after they, Dementia, and their allies defeated New Irlandia and the other combatants in the area in the Great North American War of 1750. To put it bluntly, Dementia Minor has swallowed New Arcadia, New Hibernia, New Romeania, New Asturia, and New Ruritania."

It was a complete and total victory. Sarah knew from Ben's year with Mr. Harrison that he carefully weighed the opposing sides, and usually a war resulted in some land being given up, just as the losers in European wars had to relinquish a province or two, but an entire country was rarely absorbed.

Hands shot up all over the room. Mr. Harrison called on a short girl with stringy black hair from New Arcadia in the first row.

"There are six other colonies in this area. How can *they* defeat all of *us* if there is only one of them?" she asked in a very nasal tone.

"There are several reasons why they win. First, because you are all separate. None of you have any allies and most of you revolted against your mother country and are completely independent. They have about 110,000 fighting men, including their Native American allies. This is not too high of a number, given the number of colonists in New Dementia and the number of tribes they have treaties with. I'm not even counting their other allies or any further troops Dementia might send, which would compensate for their Native American warriors being somewhat unmanageable. With 25,000 to 50,000 settlers, each of you, if I use the same ratio of combatants to noncombatants that they use, have between 2,500 and 5,000 fighting men. They could fight you in turn and crush you one by one."

From his enthusiasm, it was clear that Mr. Harrison greatly enjoyed military history, although the curriculum gave him little room to bring it into his classes.

"Even if they fought you all at once, the six of you have only about 25,000 fighting men. They still greatly outnumber you."

"But our military is mostly cavalry," a representative of New Asturia reminded Mr. Harrison.

"This is war in the forests fought largely with Native American tactics. Using cavalry would just give free horses to your enemies," Mr. Harrison said, shaking his head.

Joey Merlino, who was from Youngstown, Ohio, raised his hand. His team was Romeania, and New Romeania was equivalent to the state of Ohio. Mr. Harrison pointed to him.

"Mr. Harrison, we are still a loyal colony of Romeania. They will send us troops and weapons."

"How, Mr. Merlino? Dementia Minor has the Mississippi River closed, and you're far from New Orleans. It's difficult to cross the Alleghenies, and the East Coast is controlled by your enemies."

"Aid could come in through Canada and over the Great Lakes."

"Not a bad try, but unless Canada belongs to you, you cannot just march troops through there. You might get some supplies or weapons by that route, but first you have to get them to Canada. Dementia Minor has their mother country and other European nations on their side, which creates problems for you getting across the Atlantic. Even if you did, the Great Lakes would be blocked by New Britannia. Finally, troops and supplies would have to get to you before they crushed you."

"Let me expand on something," he continued, looking at the entire class. "A war has to have an economy to run on. All the war materials must be produced as well as the usual food and clothing. Dementia Minor is the only one in the center of the map with manufacturing, and their assumptions about what they can produce are very reasonable. When they close the Mississippi, you can't get anything in from Europe. And if your completely agricultural economies were exporting any surplus, they would cut that off, hitting you financially."

"But we have a railroad to the East Coast," Joey Merlino interjected.

"Mr. Merlino, do you know what an anachronism is?" Mr. Harrison asked with a frown.

"No, sir, I don't."

"It's a historical impossibility–like Richard the Lionheart driving a tank or flying an airplane."

Merlino looked confused.

"Railroads did not exist in 1750."

Already acknowledged as the class clown among the freshmen, Joey Merlino refused to give up.

"What if we invented railroads and then built one?"

"The project, as you will recall Mr. Merlino, is limited by basic historical facts. Besides, it would be a railroad to nowhere because their allies control the East Coast." He paused for a moment. "Do you have any other questions?"

"What if we made it an underground railroad, like they had in the North before the Civil War to help the runaway slaves escape to Canada? Then their allies won't see the tracks."

There was laughter from around the room. Mr. Harrison quickly put a stop to it.

"I'm sorry, Mr. Merlino. I should have asked whether you had any *intelligent* questions."

Another hand went up.

"Mr. Harrison, I think there's still a problem with these numbers." The person speaking, Frank Foster, was one of the smartest and most well liked freshman at the high school.

"What would that be, Frank?"

"The size of their army and their Indian allies is based on the number of settlers in New Dementia. They assume a population of half a million. It seems to me that is an unrealistic figure."

"We're Dementia Minor, and they're called Native Americans," Rob muttered.

Frank Foster turned slightly and gave Rob a look that asked "Are you always like this?"

"An interesting point, Frank. First, the total population of the other seven colonies in the area is around 250,000 people. But together they're not nearly as large, in terms of square miles, as Dementia Minor. So their population per square mile is not a lot higher than the figure the rest of you are using. Second, it's not an unreasonable number. If you look at the first census of the United States, in 1790 Pennsylvania alone had almost 435,000 inhabitants. That does not include Native Americans and only about 4,000 of the total inhabitants were slaves. I think we all agree that Pennsylvania is a lot smaller in size than Dementia Minor."

At that time all hands were down, and Mr. Harrison sensed no more objections.

"All right, ladies and gentleman. I must say, this is some very excellent work by Dementia Minor. If you still appear on the map, you are either lucky enough to be their ally or you are in uncontested territory. I'll hand back your reports tomorrow."

"Nice job, you guys," Frank Foster said in the direction of the two girls at his left.

"God, you three really kicked our butts good. How did you think of all this stuff?" Joey Merlino added, turning around to look at the girls and Rob. He held out his hand for Rob to shake.

Other heads turned and nodded.

"Thanks," the girls responded to the people near them. From then on they were known as "the History Kids" to their classmates.

"Just wait, you little asshole, until class is over," Tim Tyler growled at Rob under his breath.

Tyler and his teammates, in class and on the football field, discussed taking statecraft to another level by stuffing Rob Taylor into his locker. Unfortunately for them, Mr. Harrison had very good hearing and confronted them in the hallway after class.

"Mr. Tyler, if you and your friends even think of doing anything to Rob Taylor, I'll have you before the dean of discipline so fast, you won't know what hit you. You have a lot to learn about history. First, they completely out thought you and the other teams. That's why they won. Second, peace treaties are final, both in reality and in my class project. So I suggest you grow up and get over it."

The next morning Mr. Harrison handed her team's report back to Carrie. A red A+ was on the front page and beneath it was scribbled, "You are receiving this grade because the school does not allow me to give you anything higher. This is the best report I have seen in the many years that I've done this project in this class. It should be submitted to *Interpretations*."

Interpretations was the only journal in the United States containing papers written by high school history students. Each year the faculty asked Oak Stream students to submit deserving papers for consideration. An editorial board then reviewed the submissions and made the final acceptance decisions. The manuscripts were usually the standard term papers, written on a broad subject of the student's choice rather than for a course project.

Some of the upperclassmen who were published there, even though they were quite proud of the honor, referred whimsically to the journal as *Impersonations* because they felt they were impersonating Ph.D. historians.

"We have a shot at *Impersonations*," they said to each other at lunch a few hours later. That night they got together at Sarah's after dinner and had a small celebration with Hostess Cupcakes, which Rob and Sarah were addicted to, and milk.

Although Mr. Harrison was fairly jaundiced after more than 30 years of teaching, he went to the journal's editorial board and passionately argued for the inclusion of their project report. The editors were impressed by its quality, but balked at the fact that it was not the usual self-contained term paper. Harrison argued in return that it showed what an innovative curriculum the school had and how talented these students were because they produced something exemplary from a very structured topic. Ultimately the board agreed to publish the paper if he wrote an introduction and a critical summary discussing their colony and the resulting wars. To the great surprise of everyone involved, Mr. Harrison quickly turned in two well written pieces.

Every spring the high school held a reception to celebrate the new issue of the journal. Carrie, Rob, and Sarah stood off to one side in the teachers' lounge, feeling slightly out of place, as the upperclassmen who wrote most of the papers, including Ben Jennings, congregated in the middle. Sarah's parents were at one of the tables with Rob's mother and father. Mr. Markovitz, the chair of the history division and master of ceremonies, called the gathering to order. He wore a tweed sport coat, complemented by a battered old tie that clashed with it, and his shoes desperately needed polishing. As the students ate cookies and drank soda, he introduced each author, read the title of each paper, and briefly described the topic.

"And that ends the formalities," Mr. Markovitz announced in closing. "Please take as many copies of *Interpretations* as you like and help yourself to some more refreshments."

Everyone rose and mingled, the teachers walking from one side of the room to join the students and parents.

"Congratulations to the three of you," Mr. Harrison said as he approached.

"Thanks for your help, Mr. Harrison. I'm looking forward to reading your discussion of our paper," Rob said.

"Oh, it's just a little decoration on the already completed cake," he responded turning toward the trio's parents. "Hi, I'm Dave Harrison. Your children are on the road to becoming really fine historians."

"Getting into *Interpretations* as a freshman is quite an honor. The last two years we didn't have any freshman papers and only a few from sophomores," Mr. Markovitz added as he joined them.

"When we get home, we'll have to check whether Rob is adopted," Mr. Taylor quipped. Rob's mother, a short woman with long, straight brown hair, grimaced slightly. His father, who was in need of a shave and haircut, looked like a somewhat larger version of Rob. The flannel shirt and jeans he wore reflected his blue collar background.

"I see where you get your sense of humor from, Rob," Sarah said, turning toward her friend.

Rob smiled contentedly.

"Mr. Harrison, I have a question. Will this help us get into a really good college?" Sarah asked.

Just then Carrie's mother sailed into the room. She was a pale, stiff woman of unmistakable Puritan stock with a thin, proud face.

"Carrie won't need any help getting into college. She is going to MIT." Mrs. Wilson gave the people near her daughter only a cursory glance.

Carrie dropped her head and looked down at the floor. From birth it was assumed that she would go to MIT. Her mother and father as well as a number of her ancestors had attended MIT since the school's earliest days. One of her mother's people had even endowed a building years and years ago. She was such a legacy at MIT that it would take two separate pieces of paper to list her family connections on the application.

Mr. Markovitz recognized Mrs. Wilson by her voice alone. He had already taken more than a dozen phone calls from her regarding course choices and teacher assignments for Carrie in the future. Mrs. Wilson was notorious around the school for her abrasive manner. Mr. Markovitz and Mr. Harrison turned without saying a word and walked away.

Rob ended the awkward silence by introducing Mrs. Wilson to the other parents in the circle.

"If this is over, Carrie, we should go. I'm sure you have lots of homework to do."

"Yes, Mother." After exchanging brief good-byes they left.

"I don't think I heard the word 'congratulations' from her mouth once," Rob whispered to Sarah as they each grabbed another cookie.

"You didn't miss it, Rob. She didn't say it. She never compliments Carrie," Sarah said in the most negative of tones.

"Do you need a ride home?" Sarah's mother asked when Rob and Sarah returned.

"Thanks, Mom, but it's a nice day. I'll just walk with Rob."

"OK, see you later. Congratulations again."

"Thank you," they said one after the other.

Sarah spotted Mr. Harrison in a corner, talking to some other teachers. She was still hoping for an answer to her earlier question.

"Mr. Harrison? Will this help us get into a top university?"

"It's a nice honor, but it won't carry too much weight in that department."

"What does it take, then, to get into a place like Harvard?"

Her brother Ben already had his sights set on the Ivy League school with the most ivy.

"Sarah, their applicant pool is extremely competitive. Every year they turn down lots of students with perfect SAT scores who are at the top of their high school class." His answer was blunt but honest.

"Oh boy," she said with some concern.

3
THE CONTINENTAL DIVIDE

Carrie, Rob, and Sarah had more classes together during their sophomore year as the advanced placement (AP) and honors courses opened up to them. They also pursued the many history electives Oak Stream offered. With the freshman jitters behind them and the college selection process still in the distance, it was a relatively relaxed time.

A few days before school started Carrie learned that she had made the varsity lacrosse team, which was a tribute to her hard work during the summer, including jogging lots of lonely miles. She had played the sport for the first time during the previous year and quickly had become proficient with the long stick. A tough defender, she was also a good passer.

Before their first game, Carrie noticed that her mother was not in the stands. In many ways that was a relief. At the start of Carrie's freshman year, Mrs. Wilson had attended all the junior varsity home games and yelled to her continually whenever she was on the field. Her mother had never played the sport, even though it was very popular out East, but that didn't stop her from giving Carrie minute instructions about where to go and what to do. Almost everyone, except Mrs. Wilson, understood that this did no good, because whatever she said was probably irrelevant by the time Carrie processed the information. More than that, her comments actually did some harm because they interfered with Carrie's concentration and drowned out what her teammates were saying to each other. The varsity coach, after consulting with her junior varsity counterparts, pulled Carrie's mother aside early in the season and politely explained to her that her attempts to "help" were disruptive. Mrs. Wilson stopped coming at that point.

As Oak Stream's opponents from one of the tony Northern suburbs got off the bus and walked toward the field, their captain remarked loudly,

"I hate having to come all the way down here to play these guys."

The Oak Stream girls, in a shooting drill at the goal near the street, turned and stared at her.

"That's right; you're not on the North Shore anymore. Too bad," one of the Oak Stream captains responded loudly.

The locals all laughed.

It started out well enough as the teams traded goals early. Carrie came in late in the half as a wing defender to spell one of the seniors. The girl who made the crack coming off the bus was the forward opposite her.

"Haven't seen you before. You a sophomore?"

"Yeah," Carrie answered.

"Well then, get ready to look bad."

"In your dreams, girl. And by the way, good luck winning Miss Congeniality."

Carrie held her own in the first half as well as during the latter part of the second, when she came on again. Continually up against the same girl, Carrie largely shut down her shooting and sometimes disrupted her passing. Carrie even temporarily saved the day when she knocked the ball away from another opposing forward who came in one on one on the goalie after beating her defender.

Near the end of the game, Oak Stream's highly ranked opponents scored the deciding goal. But the coach told Carrie, "Nice job, Wilson," when she came off the field. It was the start of a successful varsity career for her.

Another development that same week was the founding of the History Club. Fresh out of college, Anne Mason, the faculty advisor, was of middle height and wore her brown hair tied back in a ponytail. She was the epitome of perky, with an enthusiastic smile that never seemed to go away. At the club's initial meeting, Sarah, Carrie, and Rob spotted Joey Merlino and Frank Foster, who had been friends since junior high, hanging around in the back of the room with a small group from their previous year's Honors American history class.

"Students, welcome and please take a seat. I'm Ms. Mason and I'll be the faculty advisor for the History Club this year. After discussing this with other members of the department, I've decided to make this a fairly active organization. What this means is that members of the club must do a short project each semester. Now, before you all get up and leave, let me tell you more about the project. It will be so much fun!" she gushed.

"The theme for this semester is Hidden Local History. Each member of the club will investigate some aspect of Oak Stream history that is more or less unknown and use original source material to shed light on it. In terms of topics, that means you can't do Hemingway or Frank Lloyd Wright, unless you're able to come up with something really new about them. Since their lives have been well documented, I suspect that's not going to happen, so you should really look elsewhere. For example, there might be an interesting house that you see every day on your way home. We all know how architecturally diverse this village is and how old some of the homes are. You could investigate the history of the house and determine when it was built, who lived there at various times, and what events happened to the occupants. What were their triumphs, joys, and sorrows?"

"But how would we do that?" a freckled, red-haired girl in her junior year wanted to know.

"That's the fun part. You're going to learn how to do historical research in the process, as opposed to sitting in a comfy chair reading history that someone else wrote. This will be invaluable to you when you're writing papers in college. Sticking with the house example, you could contact the current owners and ask to interview them briefly. In an old community, houses often have an oral history that is passed down from owner to owner. Talk to the oldest residents on that block and ask them, or any people you can find who lived on the block even earlier, the same questions. Go to the newspapers and check the address of the house. The *Chicago Tribune* is an especially good source because it is digitized, going back to its first issue, and can be searched via computer. Beyond deaths and weddings, various news items will mention the person's address. Once you have some initial names, you can piece together the entire family using genealogical records and the information in obituaries and learn more about them. You'll probably be surprised by what you find, including possibly correcting present day misconceptions, because oral history often gets distorted over time."

Although it sounded like a fair bit of work, a number of the students in the room were intrigued by the idea of doing original research.

"In terms of other projects," Ms. Mason continued, "you could do the same thing with a commercial building along Lake Street. In this case you wouldn't be focusing so much on the people who worked there, unless the owner lived in Oak Stream, but instead on what businesses operated there and what happened to them. Or you could investigate some of the people who lived in Oak Stream at one time but were not internationally famous. I understand that a number of prominent Chicagoans lived here with their families. There are also the original settlers of the area. Again, if you're going to research a person who is fairly well known, focus on what is not common knowledge about him or her. In that case, spend time on their families and their personal lives rather than on their careers."

Ms. Mason stopped for a moment to catch her breath.

"A final suggestion is the cemeteries in the neighboring suburb of Forest Home. Cemeteries are a great repository of history. In fact, many a tombstone tells a tale. If you see an intriguing monument or mausoleum, that's often the doorway to an interesting person. A good-sized mausoleum was very expensive in the old days, so that person came from some wealth. Find their obituary and then search them the same way you would the owner of a house. And keep your written reports under ten pages, please. I recognize that this is on top of your usual class work so I think you should really not go overboard on this."

The thought of exploring the local cemeteries appealed to Sarah. Ever since her father had taken her and Ben for a walk through Graceland Cemetery on Chicago's North Side, which was the final resting place of many of the city's most prominent citizens, she had been quietly interested in the ornate monuments on graves that were common in an earlier era as well as the story each one hinted at.

"Ms. Mason?" Sarah inquired. "For the project, does the deceased absolutely have to be from Oak Stream? There must be tens of thousands of people buried in Forest Home, and you really can't tell where they lived until you research them."

"That's a good point. Since there aren't any cemeteries in Oak Stream itself and the people buried in Forest Home are for eternity local residents, more or less, they are fair game for the project regardless of where they lived when they were alive."

That clinched it for Sarah. She was going to investigate the sprawling Forest Home Cemetery and, if necessary, some of the adjoining ones in the suburb of the same name.

"Is it OK to work on Ludacris?" someone in the back asked.

"Who?"

"The rapper Ludacris aka Chris Bridges. He went to school here."

"I don't think that there is enough history there for him to be a topic. Plus, is there really much that is unknown about him?"

"I have a question, Ms. Mason." Rob said, raising his hand. "There are lots of historical markers around Oak Stream, some of which are fairly obvious like the World War I memorial in Scoville Park. But some you wouldn't see unless you're right in front of them. Can I catalog all these markers in my project, giving their location, discussing what they commemorate and when they were placed?"

"That's a very acceptable project. That would make an interesting walking tour in local history. In fact, this is exactly the sort of thinking I want to encourage. There is a historical marker at the entrance of this building, commemorating the Oak Stream men who died in World War I. Did any of you ever notice it? People, there is history all around you! You just have to look for it! Every time you see something, think about the history of it. And, remember, I want you to really have fun with this!"

Fun appeared to be Ms. Mason's favorite word.

"I intend to, Ms. Mason," was Rob's response. Sarah saw the

mischievous smile on his face.

"Rob, what are you up to?" she whispered.

"Oh nothing."

"Now, it goes without mentioning that the local historical society is a valuable resource. They have the early issues of the Oak Stream newspaper as well as other information that can be of great value to you. They've agreed to help in anyway they can, but you have to call first and make an individual appointment for a research visit."

After Ms. Mason concluded, the room was abuzz for the next fifteen minutes as the club members kicked ideas back and forth.

"What do you think you're going to work on, Carrie?" Sarah asked her friend, who seemed lost in her own thoughts while she and Rob listed the markers in parks and other places they knew of.

"I think I'm going to write about prominent women in the nineteenth century in Oak Stream. There's Frances Willard, of course, who taught elementary school here when she was young. She may be right on the cusp of the famous and therefore heavily researched already, but the Women's Christian Temperance Union had a headquarters in Oak Stream so there must be some other interesting local women involved in the temperance and women's suffrage movements I can work into the paper as well. And it was a hot issue locally. I think Forest Home was actually formed as a separate suburb due to disagreements between the drys and wets in what was once greater Oak Stream."

"That sounds interesting. I suppose you'll start with books on Willard. Want to do a research trip on Saturday? We can go to the library and then swing by the cemeteries."

"Sure. I imagine you'll be on your own, Rob, looking around for markers."

"Basically, once I ask the people at the historical society what they know."

They rose to leave the room, bumping into Merlino and Foster in the hallway.

"What are you guys going to work on?" Rob asked.

"I'm not sure, but I think it will be sports related. There have been so many great teams here in the past. We've won a ton of state championships. I may investigate some of the individual players as well as a few of the teams."

"And you, Frank?"

"I'm thinking about something similar. Zuppke was the football coach at Oak Stream before he went down to U. of I. so I might look at his years here, which I think were incredibly successful."

"That's really interesting," said Rob.

That Saturday, the girls hit the Oak Stream library as soon as it opened, finding many books about Frances Willard and her world.

"This has been really productive," Carrie said as she put aside her pencil and note cards a few hours later. "If I research the newspapers and go to the historical society next, I can flesh this out some more. Want to get a sandwich before we go to the cemeteries?"

"Sure," Sarah answered as she glanced out the third floor window toward Scoville Park next to the library. "Is that Rob down there, taking a picture of the metal plaque on that rock?"

"I think it is. But he looks like he's done and moving on."

"Good, then we don't want to bother him. Let's go."

An hour later they were at the entrance to Forest Home Cemetery, near some of the most unusual graves. Preliminary research on a Web site called graveyards.com gave Sarah a summary of the more fascinating monuments and markers there. On a beautiful autumn day, they walked the cemetery for hours and, with help from the people in the office, saw almost everything there was to see.

While a few graves were interesting, Sarah was less than enthusiastic about them for the project. She dismissed the men executed for complicity in the Haymarket bombing who were buried there as too famous. Similarly, Emma Goldman and the remaining political radicals in Forest Home were found to be unsuitable. At the other extreme, she thought that the lives of young Lars and Eddie Schmidt, despite the heart wrenching monument to them, would not have been full enough to warrant the type of investigation that was called for.

"No good?" Carrie asked, recognizing Sarah's frown as they walked back to the car.

"No, no good. I don't think any of these will work for me."

"OK, let's go down to the Jewish Waldheim cemeteries at Des Plaines and Roosevelt."

"Waldheim? What does that mean?"

"It's German for 'Forest Home,'" said Carrie, who understood a bit of German. "Just as this one is called."

"Oh. I knew that," Sarah said self-deprecatingly.

They walked a few blocks south and went in the first cemetery entrance they saw, among the tangle of individual Jewish burial grounds founded by synagogues, fraternal organizations, burial societies, and groups of countrymen back in the day, at the southwest corner of the intersection across from a shopping center. When Eastern European Jews first came to Chicago, they settled in the Maxwell Street entry port on the near West Side. Those who became more affluent moved farther west on Roosevelt Road, many ending up in the Lawndale neighborhood next to Cicero. Just like the Poles, Irish, Germans, and most other immigrants, their family members were buried outside the city once Chicago frowned upon cemeteries inside its limits, usually on the shortest line that extended from their neighborhoods to the suburbs.

"How many of these little cemeteries are there?"

"A couple hundred at least."

"I'm not seeing anything too interesting in this one," Sarah responded as they walked back toward the entrance of Anshe Kanesses Israel Cemetery No. 3. Three stone columns that originally held the gate, now long gone, stood within the chain-link fence enclosing the area. A red stone plaque on the inside of one of them caught Sarah's eye. Part of it read:

> In Memoriam
> This Fence and Gate Donated and Erected in
> Affectionate Remembrance of Our Departed Friend
> Samuel J. Morton
> Died May 13, 1923

"Samuel Morton. I think I've heard of this guy."

"Who is he?"

"Unless I'm mistaken, he was a big-time bootlegger during Prohibition. He's mentioned in a book about Al Capone I read once."

"Oh, I don't think Frances Willard would have liked him very much," Carrie said shaking her head.

"Probably not."

They headed straight for the office. The woman at the desk was unaware of the plaque or whether a Samuel J. Morton was buried there. But a check of the computerized records showed that his grave was in Jewish Waldheim, in a different part along its southern border.

"Hidden history," Carrie said to Sarah, who would return the next day to visit the grave site.

Carrie dove into her project as soon as she got home. By midnight she had her note cards organized and had completed a rough outline of her paper. By Sunday afternoon she had a longer one, with facts in some places and questions that still needed to be answered in others.

Sarah returned to the library the next day to look at the book *Mr. Capone* by Robert Schoenberg. Sure enough, Samuel J. Morton was Samuel "Nails" Morton, a World War I hero, virile protector of his fellow Jews from anti-Semites, and Prohibition era gangster who was credited with showing the North Side O'Banion gang how to make a fortune from bootlegging. He was thrown from a spirited horse and kicked to death in 1923 before the Prohibition gang wars started in Chicago. The character named "Nails" Nathan in the classic gangster movie *The Public Enemy* was based on Samuel Morton.

Sarah headed back to Waldheim and found Nails's grave in a section containing a number of his relatives. Puttering around, she noticed that Maxie Eisen, another prominent member of the North Side gang, was a short distance away in the same area. She decided to call her paper "The Two Bootleggers."[1]

That evening Carrie and her mother sat at an elegant mahogany table in the cavernous, dark-paneled dining room they ate in whenever two or more had lunch or dinner together. The family never took their meals in the similarly large and newly remodeled (at great expense) kitchen, even though it had a table of its own with many chairs.

"How was school this week, Carrie?"

"Good. We had our first lacrosse game."

"I don't think I'll be going this year. I cannot abide those coaches."

Carrie mentioned the History Club and the discussion of the project requirement to her mother.

"What are you thinking about working on?"

"I'm going to do prominent local women of the nineteenth century."

"Why would you do that when you can write about this house instead? It was designed by William Drummond, who had worked for Frank Lloyd Wright at one time, and we've gone to great pains, as you well know, to maintain it in its original style while adding all the modern conveniences."

The house was a gigantic brick and stone structure, which reminded Carrie of the hall that the family had endowed at MIT. Contractors and dust had been her constant companions during the last several years as her mother had amused herself during her father's business travels by having parts of the house remodeled. The first and second floors, except for the kitchen, were maintained in the style of the period during which the house was built. The third floor, which originally had been the servants' rooms and a massive ballroom, had been completely converted. It was now divided into an office plus a billiard room and bar for her father, a study for her mother, and a soundproof theater that seated up to twenty people. The old chauffeur's quarters over the garage long ago had become a space for Carrie and her friends so that her mother would not have to hear the noise when they played.

"But, Mother, I've already started on this topic and I'm fairly far along on it."

"I know, but you have time to start over. This house is the talk of the

---

[1] Four tenths of a mile east of Des Plaines Avenue on Greenberg Road in the suburb of Forest Park stands an obelisk marking the Morton family section in the Independent Progressive Lodge Cemetery (number 93 in Jewish Waldheim). There were actually two men named Maxie Eisen who were prominent in Chicago gangland during the 1920s. The one not buried with the Mortons was a business racketeer who preyed on his fellow Jews.

neighborhood and rightfully so. It is a wonderful home for you and deserves your attention."

"Mother, I think that I should be allowed to choose my own topic," she said with more than a touch of anxiety.

"Caroline Wilson, I really must insist that you write about this house. While you may not notice it, few of your classmates live in a home like this. Let them write about the other topics since they don't have the same opportunities that you do."

"But . . ." the words died on Carrie's lips as her mother interrupted her.

"Caroline, your paper will be about the history of this house and how we've changed it. You realize, of course, that the trust fund that has been set up for you is administered until you come of age by your father and me. Its terms can be changed at any time."

Her mother always played the money card with her whenever she wasn't able to get what she wanted any other way.

"Yes, Mother," Carrie said sadly. "May I be excused from dinner? I need to start on my new topic."

She ran up to her room and threw the research materials from the past two days in the garbage can by the desk before flinging herself, in tears, on the bed.

The next day a courier arrived from downtown Chicago with the full title records for her house, which the family lawyer had pulled up after a phone call from Carrie's mother. When she canceled a trip with Sarah to the historical society so that she could speak to an expert on local architecture, Sarah asked, "Aren't you working on nineteenth century women any more?"

"No," Carrie said turning her head in the other direction, "my mother wants me to do our house."

Although Carrie disliked having the topic forced on her, her ingrained commitment to excellence took over, and she spent long hours researching the people who had lived at 312 Oak Street. Using census records and obituaries, she constructed detailed family trees and then searched for the names in the newspapers, both in the digitized *Chicago Tribune* and in the files of tattered clippings from all the Chicago papers maintained at the *Chicago Sun-Times*, the latter of which a family friend had won her access. She finished in mid-October, completing a 25-page report long after Sarah was done with her gangsters and Rob had found all the local historical markers that were evident.

Several members of the History Club responded to Ms. Mason's call for volunteers and did presentations in late October. Among the sophomores, Frank Foster focused on Zuppke's three years as the football coach, emphasizing the high school national championships his teams won each year but also analyzing whether a number of the innovations usually credited to him were in fact introduced earlier or simultaneously by other coaches. Joey Merlino revealed that the "national" championships in 1910, 1911, and 1912 were mythical, because Oak Stream, regarded as the best team in the Chicago area, faced representative teams from the East or West coasts in invitational contests that obviously did not pair the two best teams in the country each year. He also discussed some of the star players on those teams, such as Bart Macomber, who followed Zuppke to Illinois, and Paul "Pete" Russell, the quarterback on the University of Chicago's 1913 national championship team. Because everyone likes a good gangster story, the audience listened with great interest as Sarah talked about the bootleggers buried nearby. She also revealed that the horse involved in Nails Morton's death may in reality not have been executed in revenge by his gangster pals because there was no mention of it in the newspapers until long after the event.

Carrie's talk, entitled "312 Oak: The Story of a Home," started out well enough. Unlike the others, she did a PowerPoint presentation with exterior photos of the house that immediately got everyone's attention. Carrie tantalized the audience with various tidbits about the previous owners, from the wealthy industrialist who had it built in the mid-1920s before losing his fortune in the Great Depression to the mob-connected lawyer who had owned it during the 1950s and 1960s. After raising his children there, the attorney divorced his high school sweetheart and installed his much younger (and blonder) mistress in her place. She went after him with a butcher knife one day when she learned he was, in turn, replacing her with a redhead 10 years her junior. He later sold the house to a doctor who was followed by several owners who were doctors and lawyers.

Carrie then revealed that her family owned the house. She looked at the ground as opposed to the audience as she displayed, room by room, how it had been renovated. The listeners, many of whom lived in small brick bungalows and similar sized stucco houses in south Oak Stream, found the topic pretentious.

"So this is where the Rockefellers live," one of them cracked.

Carrie sat down quickly, to muted applause, just as Rob rose to give his presentation. Following Ms. Mason's suggestion, Rob had organized the historical markers into two walking tours, covering separate parts of Oak Stream and discussed them in that order. The exception was the sign that he kept for the end of his talk.

"Finally, I want to mention what is, in my opinion, a historical marker because it refers to an earlier point in time. That's the sign on Chicago Avenue by the high school denoting the ridge that runs north and south through Oak Stream as the Continental Divide–the sign that says that rain east of the ridge goes into the Great Lakes via the Chicago River and from there into the Atlantic Ocean while water west of the ridge ends up in the Mississippi River and ultimately the Gulf of Mexico. But, since the flow of the Chicago River was reversed in 1900, that water goes down the sanitary canal into the Des Plaines, Illinois, and Mississippi rivers. Besides sending our sewage and other pollution to central Illinois and St. Louis, doesn't this mean that our beloved ridge is no longer a Continental Divide?"

Joey Merlino, who sensed where Rob was going, immediately cracked up.

"I really think that, in the interest of historical correctness, this marker needs to be taken down."

"Very good, Rob," Ms. Mason chirped enthusiastically with out a clue that Rob was going to tweak the village's nose on this subject. "I'm sure we all enjoyed that."

The next week there was quite a lot of gossip in the sophomore class about Carrie and her house. Fortunately, Sarah was watching Carrie's back. When a girl in the lunchroom made a comment about "Princess Carrie" and "the castle she lives in", Sarah immediately called her out.

"Chelsea," Sarah remarked in the hallway in a low voice. "I'm not sure what you heard from the History Club, but Carrie did not want to do that topic."

"Really? I heard she went on and on about her multi-million dollar house," Chelsea Milton said in her own defense.

"Only because her mother made her do it. She was working on women's issues until this was forced on her."

"I didn't know that."

"I know you didn't. Chelsea, I want to tell you that Carrie's really down to earth even though her family is wealthy."

Although it took a bit of work, between Rob and Sarah the word spread that Carrie was quite unpretentious. It helped that Chelsea Milton, who was very popular, made a point of being friendly to Carrie in public after that and retracted her previous comments when people asked her about them.

A week later an op-ed piece written by Rob ran in the *Midweek Beacon*, the local paper most interested in the village's heritage. He argued that the sign about the Continental Divide was incorrect and should be taken down. It caused quite a bit of controversy, as tempests in teapots often will, and evoked numerous letters in response over the next few weeks. The village board, wanting to play it safe, held an open forum to discuss the issue before making a decision.

The board of trustees, like the village itself, was divided along certain lines. Many of the residents who had lived there for years were members of a group called the Good Old Oak Streamers or GOOS for short. They believed that Oak Stream before 1960 had been a model of perfection and wanted to keep things that way. While they focused primarily on historical preservation, their political influence was strong enough to elect two people to the board, both of whom belonged to the Conservative Party.

Members of the Progressive Citizens Committee (PCC) were mostly newer residents who disagreed with the GOOS on quite a few issues. The PCC, given its size, was able to put two members of the Progressive Party on the village board. The two trustees who were political independents and the seventh trustee from the Green Party more often than not lined up with the Progressives, but had their own views in general, which made them non-partisan. It made for some interesting meetings as the Conservatives and Progressives jostled with each other to win the other trustees to their side.

When Rob walked into the meeting room at the village hall, it was already packed with people. The vice president of the GOOS, Myra Campbell, who attended every board meeting, had arrived half an hour early and was standing at the microphone in the audience section so that she could be the first person to speak. Her pearl necklace danced in the beams from the overhead lights against the background of her long, dark blue dress. Jerry Carlson, a political independent who served as president of the board, called the meeting to order at the scheduled time.

"Ladies and gentlemen, this is a public forum so that the citizens of Oak Stream can give us their input on the suggestion that a certain sign in the village be taken down. Is Robert Taylor here? I think it would be best if Mr. Taylor speaks first."

"Mr. President, I object," Myra Campbell called out in her shrill, 80-year-old voice.

"To what, Mrs. Campbell?"

"I arrived early in order to be able to speak first. You are denying me my First Amendment rights of free speech."

"Mrs. Campbell, no one is denying you the right to speak. I am simply suggesting that to be expeditious, since Mr. Taylor raised this issue and has some information on it, we should begin with him. You will be allowed to speak in time."

"If I do not speak first I will sue you and the board. I will take this all the way to the United States Supreme Court."

"As you have many times, Mrs. Campbell," Mr. Carlson said matter of factly, "although the highest court in the land has refused to hear any of your lawsuits. Are you willing to let Mr. Taylor speak first, if you go after him?"

"No, I am not."

"Well then, as the chair, it is my ruling that Robert Taylor be allowed to make the first public comments. Those who object may pursue whatever legal remedies they wish."

The onlookers were surprised by Rob's youth because the average age of those in the audience was over 50. Rob reiterated his views from the *Midweek Beacon* piece and then returned to his seat at the back of the room.

Myra Campbell, weighing 130 pounds in all, almost plowed him over as she rose from her chair.

"There are certain standards in Oak Stream that must be maintained. The ridge should still be called the Continental Divide because it's always been that way. That sign must stay!"

The two Conservative Party members at the trustees' table nodded in agreement.

The PCC was solidly behind Mrs. Campbell–if not intellectually at least physically. One PCC member after another followed her and voiced the opinion that, in terms of accuracy, the sign was no longer acceptable and must come down. The GOOS in the queue exchanged uncertain glances because they knew they had little to say beyond repeating Myra Campbell's demand. The Progressive Party trustees smiled faintly, sensing victory.

A short, portly man who resembled an owl came unwittingly to the aid of the GOOS.

"My name is Norm Peterson," he began. "I know there is some strong disagreement here and I don't want to get involved in that debate. I just want to talk about the facts for a moment. Mr. Taylor has asserted that since 1900 all the water from east of the ridge has gone into the Gulf of Mexico, just like the water from the west side. Is this really true? Can you prove that all the water in the Chicago River goes down the Mississippi ultimately and not a single drop goes into the lake? If that's incorrect, then his entire premise is wrong."

"That's right," Mrs. Campbell shouted as loudly as her voice would allow. "This is bad science."

The GOOS in the line nodded in agreement.

"Myra," Jerry Carlson admonished, "so that everyone is allowed to voice their opinion, I must insist that until all those who wish to speak have had their chance, no one else speaks. There will be time later for additional comments."

Looking around the room, he expected that it would be a long meeting.

"This is censorship. I object."

"No, it is you once again disrupting a meeting of this body. If you don't keep quiet I will have the Sergeant at Arms remove you from the room."

"You're discriminating against me!"

"Officer, please remove Mrs. Campbell," Jerry Carlson said to the Oak

Stream policeman who was there to keep order.

Officer Brandenburg escorted her to his squad car and drove her home, just as he had done for about a third of the board meetings during the last two years. The ride in the police car was the highlight of her week.

"Now that the meeting can be conducted in an orderly fashion," Carlson said once Mrs. Campbell was gone, "let's hear from the next person in line."

"There is a gate where the river meets Lake Michigan," a tall, bearded African American man said before Mr. Peterson had gone very far up the aisle. "Doesn't that keep the river water out of the lake?"

Several of the board members looked at Jerry Carlson.

"Since this is related to Mr. Peterson's statement, I think we should allow Mr. Peterson to respond. But I remind everyone to please wait to be recognized before speaking. Mr. Peterson?"

The last speaker moved to one side as Peterson returned to the head of the line.

"Yes, there is a gate there, but it's not a wall. River water can still get into the lake. And that gate is opened up every time a boat goes from the river into the lake or vice versa."

"I don't know your name, sir," Carlson asked the man who had raised the issue and looked eager to reply.

"My name is Milton Bishop."

"Mr. Bishop, do you have a further comment?"

"Yes, I do. If the river is running in the other direction, then it seems to me that the gate may not be the important thing after all. It may just be keeping more lake water from flowing into the river and down the Mississippi as opposed to vice versa."

"I looked into this issue quite a bit before I came here tonight, Mr. Bishop," Peterson said after being acknowledged. "A study by the University of Illinois in 2005 shows that the current on the surface of the river may be in the direction of the sanitary canal, but the current could be going toward the lake below the surface. It may be bidirectional. And therefore water from the Chicago River still does flow toward the lake."

Milton Bishop seemed satisfied by the answer and sat down.

The next person in line, a civil engineer with red bushy hair, challenged Norm Peterson as soon as he was able to speak. "Mr. Peterson, I've looked at this as well. Chicago regularly lets millions of gallons of water flow from the lake into the river. So it seems to me that whatever does go into the lake just comes right back out again. It heads south, and therefore Mr. Taylor is most likely correct that none of the water east of the ridge currently goes in the Atlantic Ocean."

Jerry Carlson, a businessman whose small printing company was struggling, was lost in the details. He wondered if he really should be spending so much of his time as a trustee when the issues were often of this magnitude.

"That's your opinion," Peterson shot back. "You don't know how much water gets into the lake and flows just as it always did."

"And your comments are just your opinion," the other man fired back. "The U of I study is clearly only a theoretical modeling of the flow of the river."

"Order, order!" Carlson called out.

Sitting in the back of the room, Rob Taylor smiled contentedly.

The rest of the people waiting to be heard came up and voiced their opinions, many of them along party lines.

"Ladies and gentlemen, I believe everyone who wishes to speak has been able to. Is that correct?" Jerry Carlson said some time later as the line evaporated. "Then I would like to thank you all for your input. We have heard a number of divergent views. I would like to see if we can now find some common ground. For example, are we—meaning those of us in this room—able to agree that since 1900 not all of the water east of the ridge goes into Lake Michigan and east from there?"

A group of GOOS caucused in the back reaches of the room. They were happy to concede that not all the water in the Chicago River went in that direction. This allowed the ridge to still be of importance, and worthy of a sign, because the flow of water might on average be different on the two sides of the crest.

"In turn, to put some further bounds on the discussion tonight, can we agree that not all the water from the east side of the ridge goes down the sanitary canal and ends up in the gulf?"

"May we have a minute please, Mr. Carlson?" the ranking member of the PCC asked.

The PCC members went off to the left side of the room and had an animated discussion. A few moments later the man voiced their opinion. "Mr. Chairman, the people I've spoken to all believe that based on what's been said tonight that there is no clear proof that any of the water from the Chicago River goes into the Atlantic Ocean via the Great Lakes. We believe it all goes into the gulf."

"We disagree," a GOOS shouted out.

At that point an electrical engineer suggested that the village perform a test to settle the issue. If a number of microchips, of the type used in tracking systems, were placed in water tight capsules and dropped into the north branch of the Chicago River, it could be determined weeks later where they ended up. That sparked another hour of debate about how close to reality the simulation was and how many chips would have to be used, given the chance of loss or damage, to get reliable results.

Ken Roberts, the Green Party member on the board, spoke next.

"People, it sounds like this could get expensive. Who knows how many times it will have to be run until you get it right? If all the capsules are the same, they'll all be at the same level of the river, such as floating on the top, and then you won't allow for the possibility that the current below the surface may go in the opposite direction from the one on the surface. I believe firmly in the conservation of resources, including the taxpayers' money, and therefore I can't agree to this."

The chair saw several board members nod in agreement.

Rob smiled to himself again.

"Ladies and gentlemen, given the lateness of the hour, I think we should conclude this forum. The board will meet in closed session in one week to discuss the issue further."

When the board convened again, there was strong opposition to spending any money to determine where the Chicago River water really went. In fact, the Green Party member and the independents felt that the whole thing was getting out of hand, which left the Progressives without their usual allies. So clearly they could not pass a motion to have the sign taken down. On the other hand, there had been so much commotion that the board felt that it had to do something, especially after holding a public hearing at which everyone agreed that the direction of the river had changed somewhat in 1900. Ken Roberts eventually suggested a simple compromise. The board could change the wording on the sign to say "This ridge is commonly referred to as the Continental Divide," which gave both sides something of a victory. The sign and the traditional label for the ridge would stay, but the term "Continental Divide" was treated as a figure of speech. The motion passed by a vote of six to zero, with one abstention, which was the closest thing to unanimity at a board meeting that anyone could remember.

During the December school break, the principal at the high school pulled Anne Mason aside and gently suggested that it would be good if the history projects did not kick up quite so much dust around town. She decided that next semester's theme would be more national in character to avoid a recurrence of the problem.

"This term the projects will be on the connections between local and national history," she announced at the first meeting in February. "For example, World War I was an important national issue. You could look at what percentage of young men in Oak Stream served in the military and also what the casualty rate was compared to the national average. Or, you could examine how people in the village supported the war effort while the boys were off fighting."

"I have a question, Ms. Mason."

"Yes, Rob," she said with some trepidation.

"When I was going around last semester looking for the markers I noticed signs in Oak Stream declaring it to be a nuclear weapon free zone. What exactly does that mean? Is that symbolic, or is it enforced, and are people penalized for violating the ordinance? What if I bought an old nuclear missile from someone in the former Soviet Union, where I hear these things can be obtained, and walked around downtown with it? Would I get arrested?"

"Thank you for sharing that with us," she said in an attempt to cut him off.

"If I get convicted, is there a fine? Or could I get sent to jail? Someone really needs to clarify this. And then there are larger national issues. If the federal government decided to build a missile base, with nuclear warheads, in Oak Stream, could the village stop them? Or would Oak Stream have to secede from the Union? That was tried before, in 1861, and didn't work out so well. If Oak Stream did secede, would we all be drafted into its army and end up fighting the federal troops? Would we have to wear gray uniforms?"

Sarah grimaced as the boys in the back of the room convulsed with laughter.

"That is quite enough, Mr. Taylor!" Ms. Mason said to him irritably.

"Can I work on this as my project this semester, Ms. Mason? I think there are a number of interesting legal, practical, and moral issues here."

"No, you may not."

"That's not fair. It fits the description."

"I forbid you from working on that topic!" Anne Mason screamed as she stormed out of the room.

To everyone's surprise, Mr. Harrison showed up at the start of the club's next meeting. He tossed a folder on the lectern and opened it.

"Ladies, gentlemen," he said before he turned to look directly at Rob, "and the rest of you. Ms. Mason has taken on some new duties in the department so I am replacing her as the club's advisor. There is a change in plans. Instead of doing projects, I will choose a book that we will discuss once you've had a chance to read it—something a bit removed from Oak Stream, such as Gibbon's *The History of the Decline and Fall of the Roman Empire*, which I'm sure you'll all enjoy."

"Gee, thanks, Rob," Carrie said in his direction.

Rob smiled apologetically.

4
THE GRADUATION PARTY

"Dad, can I invite some of my friends to Ben's graduation party?" Sarah asked two weeks before the end of the school year.

"Honey, of course you can. By the way, it's not just Ben's graduation party; it's a family celebration."

"Call it what you want, but it's still Ben's party, and all his friends will be there."

"Do you feel left out?"

"No, it's not that. It's just that they're his friends and since they're two years ahead of me, they'll be talking mostly about what colleges they're going to, and I won't have anything to add to the conversation."

"Kevin is bringing a couple of friends. How many do you want to invite?"

"Just Rob and Carrie."

One of the valedictorians among the graduating seniors at Oak Stream, Ben had been accepted by every college he applied to and was going to Harvard in the fall. Beyond his strong grades, "fives" on numerous AP exams, 99th percentiles on board exams and being a National Merit Finalist, Ben had a ton of extracurriculars. He had played soccer for four years and was a captain and had been all conference for two years. He also had volunteered at the local historical society and worked at a hardware store for a couple of summers. A regular on the math team all four years, Ben was one of the reasons that the team finished in the top five in the state three times. In national math competitions, he had received nearly perfect scores on the written exams in the last two years.

His friends at the party would include members of the math team, most of the school's several valedictorians, and other kids he knew from

AP classes, and a bunch of the soccer guys. With Sarah's father's family in town and many of her mother's family living a short drive from Chicago, the relatives would be there in abundance. Many of those who lived outside the Midwest were coming in because the family was close.

The party was held on a Saturday in their large backyard, behind the big, brightly painted and now fully restored Victorian home that their parents had fallen in love with some years ago. When the caterers finished setting up, the relatives started to drift in. Ben's less abstemious friends, of whom there were only a few, were off somewhere secluded having a beer before the party because it was well known that the alcohol was only for adults.

Sarah's brother Kevin and his two friends ran back and forth from the house to the garage, shooting each other with squirt guns and periodically reloading.

"Don't get any of the adults wet, you guys," Sarah called to them. She wore a green sun dress and sandals.

"We'll use the garden hose for that," Kevin shouted to her over his shoulder.

"You do and you better hope Mom or Dad can save you, you little goosebrain. Some of Ben's friends will flatten you." Ever since he'd been a toddler, she had called her younger brother "goosebrain" whenever she was being playful with him.

As she turned away from the squirt-gun fight, Sarah saw Carrie and Rob arrive. As fitted the occasion, Carrie was well attired in a pretty red dress. Rob's idea of dressing up was to wear his better pair of jeans with an unbuttoned (and wrinkled) dress shirt over his T-shirt.

"Hey," she said to them.

"Hey," they answered one after another.

"I see we're not fashionably late," Rob offered.

"The relatives, neighbors, and other adults should all be here soon. Ben's friends will swoop down on us probably in the next hour."

"Ah, all of Oak Stream's valedictorians will be in one place. I'm sure it will be a very highbrow conversation."

"Rob, that's kind of caustic. Look in the mirror sometime. You are them. You're just as smart as they are," Carrie said. She was sensitive to criticism, even if not directed at her.

"Maybe I'm just as smart, but by the standard measures I'm not as good. All the valedictorians are straight-A students, Carrie. After two years I already have three B's and surely will get some more. Oak Stream's science department in particular seems to be convinced that I deserve nothing higher. So don't expect me to be on the stage speaking when we graduate," Rob replied.

"Not me either," Carrie said. "I'm way too right-brained to excel in

33

math. The A I got in algebra is one of the great mysteries of mankind. And you know how hard I have to work to do well in science. Gee, I just can't wait to take physics, where the two come together."

Sarah nodded in sympathy. She had received a B in two classes so far.

"I'm what I describe as a 95 percenter," Rob said in a moment of self-reflection. "My board scores are at the 95th percentile or slightly above and my class rank will be in the top five percent or so when we graduate. The fact that I'm really strong in history means I might outshine the 99 percenters, possibly even your brother Ben, in that one area, but they dominate me in everything else."

He paused for a moment.

"I might apply to Harvard, but I would need a ton of luck to get in."

"Guys, this is making me a little uncomfortable—not because you've said anything wrong, but because we're here to have a good time. We have two more years of high school, so can we please worry about this college stuff later?" Sarah asked, putting a hand to her forehead.

Sarah had a hard time when faced with even fairly simple choices, much less complex ones. She often fretted over minor things, picking one alternative and then second-guessing herself for days about it. Procrastination had become a habit, which she got away with because no major decisions had been required of her up to this point in life.

They dropped the subject for the moment, but it lay only slightly below the surface. A few minutes later Ben noticed the trio and walked over.

"Congratulations, Ben," Sarah said, reaching up to give him a hug.

"Thank you," he responded and turning from his sister said, "and thanks for coming guys. You look very nice, Carrie, while you, on the other hand, look like hell, Rob."

Rob and Ben were, despite Ben's last comment, quite friendly. Rob had loaned Ben a number of books on military history for a paper he'd written on the Crusades for AP European history during the past year and had helped him through numerous edits.

"I'll miss you, Ben. You're the best older brother a girl could have."

"It's not a big deal. I'll be home during the summers. Plus, you may be at Harvard yourself in a couple of years."

"Actually, we were just talking about that, and I would have to say 'not likely.' Academically you're off the charts, in the top five per cent of the people in the 99th percentile, and you stand out even in Harvard's applicant pool. I'm probably below their average applicant. Even your extracurriculars are great while mine are so-so. I'm a good cross-country runner, who probably won't get any faster because my body will change soon, and I've been involved in some clubs and done some volunteering."

Sarah chafed at the thought of attending a school a lot weaker academically than Harvard.

"Yes, but there are lots of other Ivy League schools," her paternal grandfather, known as Grandpa Fred to the family, said as he walked up with Grandma Mary. "There's Brown, for example, where your father went."

"The Ivy League schools aren't the only universities in existence, Sarah," Grandma Mary said. "There are fine Catholic universities throughout the country also."

Grandma Mary came from an Irish Catholic family. A number of Mary Jennings's aunts and uncles had been nuns and priests.

"So the Ivy League schools are good as well as the Catholic schools," Sarah summarized.

"Sarah, there's only one Ivy League. The education is superb, and the contacts you make are also important. It doesn't just open doors for you; it removes walls and other obstructions. You become a 'Harvard Man' or a 'Yale Man,' as they used to say when those were all male institutions. You're part of an elite club because you fit in, and that really counts for something. Trust me; it will be important for Ben."

The speaker was her uncle Joe, her father's brother. He lived in Manhattan, worked at a major investment bank, and was married to her aunt Stephanie, who had invented conspicuous consumption. She was just walking up to the group in her overly expensive designer dress with Versace heels and a Gucci bag, which she swung at her side.

"I don't know . . . I mean really, there *used* to be only one Ivy League. Now there are lots of schools in that 'league.' For example, there's Stanford on the West Coast. Sarah, you can go to class and hit the beach and the slopes all in the same week if not the same *day* if you work at it."

Her mother, from whom Sarah inherited her sense of humor, once remarked that Aunt Stephanie was the only person on the planet who spoke in italics.

"Why does everyone have to go so far away to college nowadays?" her grandma Alice asked. "Your mother went to Notre Dame and lived at home with us on the farm."

"And it's a Catholic university," Grandma Mary added.

"Times have changed, Alice," her grandpa George remarked. "They're very busy at college and it's easier to live on the campus. But there must be some other good universities in the Midwest, even if Sarah doesn't live at home."

"There are, Grandpa. Both Northwestern and the University of Chicago are right here. You think I should try to get into one of those two?"

"Some of the rest of you might disagree," Sarah's uncle Bob said, glancing at his sister-in-law Stephanie, before Grandpa George could respond, "but you don't have to go to a private school to get a good education. There are plenty of very good schools in the Big Ten besides Northwestern, such as Michigan and Wisconsin. In fact, I would say they're all very good."

"My firm, for example, does not hire any undergraduates from those schools. But we recruit at most of the Ivies." It was Bob's brother Joe speaking.

Sarah glanced at Rob, who glanced at Carrie. Carrie looked back at Sarah, trying to make sense of the discussion.

Uncle Bob, who felt that there were not only other but better jobs than being an investment banker, turned his head slightly. "Joe, there are jobs in lots of other fields than investment banking—fields that many college graduates go into."

Sarah considered fleeing from this circle and joining a group of Ben's friends. Unfortunately, they were all talking about which universities they were going to in the fall. Some of the more smug ones were bragging about how they were going to 'rock the place' once they got there. There was a fair bit of bantering back and forth about which school was better.

"I think the overall point, Sarah, which may also be what Bob is saying, is that there are many fine schools out there." The remark came from Uncle Bill, her mother's brother, who had just walked into the backyard. "Take a look at the South, for instance. Duke is one of the most selective universities in the country. Then there's Virginia and also Georgetown in Washington, D.C."

Before Grandma Mary could add that Georgetown was a Jesuit institution, someone else entered the conversation.

"That's just a part of the South," Jane, the wife of Sarah's uncle Bill, interjected. She had been born and raised in Georgia, not far from Atlanta. "If you look at the area more broadly, there are a lot of great schools. For example, there's Emory in Atlanta. As you go west, there's Tulane in New Orleans, Texas at Austin, Rice, and SMU. If you go north, there's Vanderbilt and also Washington University in St. Louis, but Missouri is a state that was always very 'Southern.' There's more to the South than just Duke."

"Oh, so there are good schools in the East, the Midwest, and the South."

"If you want to open it up more broadly, Sarah, you should consider schools in the Southwest and California. There's Arizona and UCLA and Southern Cal. Really, you could make a case for some of the California schools, like San Diego, being almost as strong as Berkeley or UCLA," Uncle Bill said.

"So, Uncle Bill, the schools you just mentioned—are they as good as the Ivy League schools, Stanford, and the other top schools in the country?"

Before he could answer, Mrs. Winters, who was in Sarah's mother's book club, gave her opinion. "They're not bad, Sarah, but a bright girl like you should really go to a traditional women's college, such as Vassar or Smith. Those are excellent schools with great atmosphere."

"Let me think about that some more, Mrs. Winters. Those sound like interesting places."

Carrie and Rob drifted off to other corners of the yard in search of appetizers, lemonade, and peace and quiet. As they left, Todd Carlson, a successful attorney who lived three doors down from the Sarah's family, walked over. He had been a Rhodes Scholar some twenty years before.

"If you want tradition and atmosphere, you should think about Oxford or Cambridge. They are the finest universities on earth. In the process, you'll get outside the U.S. and get an entirely new perspective on the world."

"They weren't founded by Henry the Eighth, were they, Mr. Carlson?" Grandma Mary asked.

"No, madam, they are much older than that."

Mary Jennings seemed relieved that they pre-dated the Reformation.

"Well, if you're considering European universities," Otto Ziegenfuss, an elderly gentleman from across the street, said, "I would really encourage you to look at Heidelberg and Tubingen. You'll get a much different world perspective on the continent than in England because the U.S. and Britain are similar in many ways. Also, the European economy is a brand new ball game, and the Germans are in the driver's seat. They have the best links to the former Soviet Bloc countries."

"That was Tubing and Heidelbingen?" Sarah asked. They sounded like German water sports to her.

"Do you speak German, Sarah?" someone else in the crowd inquired sympathetically.

"Nope, not a single word."

"That's not a problem. She still has time to learn," Mr. Ziegenfuss answered confidently. "Just remember, in the German language the verb always comes at the end of the sentence."

As other people wandered in, they recommended institutions in the Northwest and the Rocky Mountains to Sarah, along with liberal arts schools in the Midwest, such as Oberlin, Carleton, and Macalester. After a while she walked away with a curt, "Excuse me for a moment."

Sarah retreated to the front steps of the house, which were shaded by a large oak tree. Rob saw where she was headed and joined Sarah a few moments later. She was sitting alone, her head on her knees, with her hands covering her ears.

"So, Sarah, have you decided where you're going to college?" he asked as he sat down next to her.

"If I hear the word 'college' again today, my head will explode. I'm going to Stanford. No, Harvard. No, Northwestern. No, it's Duke. No, wait, Wash. U. in St. Louis or maybe Michigan or Wisconsin. No, let's make that Yale or possibly NYU if not Columbia or Carnegie Mellon or MIT or someplace in Europe I've never heard of." She went on for another minute in a mocking tone.

"Have I left anyone out?" she finally asked.

"Only the Madame Zelda School of Beauty, but it's not a four-year institution so you really shouldn't consider it."

"Well, maybe I could major in manicures there. Do they have any scholarship money?"

Carrie walked up with a cup of iced lemonade.

"Here, I brought you this. Are you OK?"

"No, I'm not OK. This college stuff is driving me crazy." Sarah took a long sip from the cup.

"I don't blame you. I couldn't stand listening to it for more than a few minutes, and they weren't even talking to me."

"I wish I didn't have to make a decision about this."

"Unfortunately, Sarah, as difficult as this is, you will have to decide. Just like the rest of us," Rob reminded her. "Can we get out of here? It will do you good, and we can talk. Is my house OK?"

He lived a few blocks north, which was on Carrie's way home. Sarah told her parents a story about something they needed to help Rob with before they left the party.

In Rob's room they cleared away part of the mess on the floor so Carrie and Sarah could sit. Rob hopped on the bed and leaned against the wall.

"Sarah, we've all got to face this. We'll be juniors next year and the process starts that early," Rob pointed out. "Let's begin at the beginning. What are we going to major in? I notice no one asked that when they were recommending places for you to go."

"For me, it's history. That's the only thing it could be," Sarah said decidedly.

"And me," Rob added.

"I don't know. What jobs can we get? Shouldn't we consider something else?"

"Carrie, we don't have to worry about that right now. With a history degree you can get a law degree or M.B.A. after that if you're concerned about money. Or go into public policy. Or continue on in history and teach with a master's degree or a Ph.D. You have lots of choices."

"It's history then for me, too," Carrie answered, reassured by the multiple prospects Rob laid out for her.

"What do you think are our chances of getting into a top university, like the schools people were throwing around at the party? I have to tell you, I'm really nervous about this. My brother got into all these prestigious places and I might not get into a single one. In comparison to Ben, I'll end up looking like the village idiot," said Sarah.

"It's a crap shoot for all of us. No offense meant, but academically we're all 95 percenters. And there's nothing in our extracurricular activities that really differentiates us from other applicants. I've got Model U. N., some tutoring at school, and volunteer work, which makes me similar to you, Sarah, except I don't have a varsity sport. Carrie, you've got lacrosse as a sport, Scholastic Bowl, Math Team, some clubs, and lots of volunteer work. But we haven't solved the world hunger problem, split atoms in our rooms, or found a cure for cancer."

"But we'll all get letters of recommendation from Mr. Harrison," Sarah observed. "Ms. Smith will write us strong letters, too."

Ms. Smith was their teacher in Honors world history this year and also taught AP European history, which they would take as seniors. She was a winner of the Golden Apple award for excellence in teaching and one of the most respected teachers at the high school.

"Plus, Rob, your paper on trade in the Roman Empire got into *Impersonations* this year, so you are two for two, and we should all have some more hits there during the next two years."

"Fair enough; we're 99 percenters in history. But Mr. Harrison is rumored to not write very good letters, and sixty students each year ask Ms. Smith, so unless she says we walk on water, we won't really shine there either," Rob offered. "We're just not going to stand out in a really top school's applicant pool. We have to apply to a few of them and hope we get lucky somewhere."

"Agreed," Carrie replied. "Although, Rob, I have to say this to you. You're what, one-eighth Potawatomi? Check the Native American box on the application, and then see how many of the top schools admit you. There won't be a lot of people in that category who are as strong as you are. You'll probably get a scholarship."

"Thanks, but no thanks."

"If you insist." Carrie's family believed strongly in using what life had given you, including your connections, to get ahead.

"If we can get back on track here, which schools? There are lots of good history departments out there. This still doesn't tell me which ones to apply to," Sarah pleaded.

"Well I don't know about you guys, but I'm going to pick seven or eight of the top programs and apply there."

"And if they don't admit you, Mr. Ninety-five Percenter? Those are probably all 'reach' schools for you," Carrie reminded him of his own argument.

"I'm also applying to the University of Illinois as my 'safety' school."

"Not a bad plan. I have some location preferences, so I'm going to take a close look at this before I apply anywhere."

"Carrie, I thought it was all set that you were going to MIT," Sarah remarked.

"Except that I haven't applied or been admitted," Carrie responded with a look of concern on her face. "I have to consider other schools. It would be unrealistic to look at it as a done deal."

Rob and Sarah nodded, although they were both convinced that Carrie would end up at MIT.

"Guys, this is really hard for me. I don't think you have any idea how my mother is about MIT. Because a hall there is named after one of her ancestors, she thinks it's the only university on earth. Every sentence about college is prefaced with, 'When you're at MIT.' And you had better not ever mention Harvard in front of her. She really hates that place. I think she dated a Harvard guy when she was an undergraduate and he dumped her for no apparent reason."

As bright and competent as Carrie was, she was very insecure. Unlike many girls, she did not polish her fingernails because she regularly bit them. Her mother was continually after Carrie to get better grades and criticized her a great deal. Mrs. Wilson especially did not like the idea of Carrie dating during high school, because in her opinion the boys were not likely to go to MIT, and the relationship would, therefore, not last. Although she never said much to Rob, Carrie confided to Sarah that her own mother drove her crazy. Her father, a successful engineer, was overly focused on his career and left the family details largely to his wife.

"OK, Sarah, what about you?" Rob asked.

"I really don't know. There are so many good schools out there. How do I know which ones to apply to?"

Carrie and Rob looked at each other with a bit of concern. They had experienced her indecisiveness numerous times. Waiting five minutes to get ice cream because Sarah was unable to choose a flavor was a common occurrence. Carrie remembered shopping trips during which Sarah had spent an hour deciding whether to buy an outfit, only to return it two days later and then buy it again the next time they were in the store.

"You have to decide, Sarah," Rob said.

5
SARAH PROCRASTINATES

Rob could be incredibly serious when he wanted to be, and in the search for a college he wanted to be. By the start of junior year, he had already made significant progress. Using the *U.S. News and World Report* rankings of graduate programs in history–there seemed to be no undergraduate rankings, but he viewed the program qualities as similar–and a Web site on which aspects of history programs could be weighted, he came up with two top 25 lists. The top 10 schools on each list were very similar. Leaving out the University of Chicago because he wanted to go farther away than the South Side of Chicago, he decided to apply to Yale, Princeton, Berkeley, Harvard, Stanford, Columbia, Michigan, and Johns Hopkins plus Illinois (his safety school).

Rob would make all his campus visits junior year, during Christmas, spring break, and a few long weekends. There were kids from Oak Stream at many schools so it was fairly easy to find a place to crash for a few days. He decided to submit all his applications as soon as possible to get the tedious part out of the way.

Carrie started with the same information as Rob and then narrowed her list down. She focused on nineteenth century American history due in part to the AP American history course they were taking junior year. Carrie also talked to students at various universities and looked at the courses offered each term because she was concerned about what was actually available and whether the senior faculty taught undergraduate courses or not.

After careful investigation, she picked Berkeley, Yale, Princeton, Stanford, Columbia, Johns Hopkins, and MIT as her choices outside the Midwest. Chicago was added to her reach schools, and she chose Michigan

41

and Illinois as safety schools, despite her desire to get far away from her mother. Carrie planned to make campus visits during her junior year–at least to the places she had never seen before. She had been on the MIT campus so many times with her family that she knew it intimately. Another visit next year to sit in on some classes would be sufficient.

Predictably, Sarah had trouble deciding. She got off on the wrong foot by calling various relatives, figuring that they had a better perspective because they could view academic choices in hindsight. They largely reiterated what they had said before. By the end of her junior year, she still did not have a short list. Sarah decided to talk to Ms. Smith, who had written an essay about the college search process and was a willing mentor to her students.

"What's bothering you, Sarah?" Jessica Smith asked as they sat in her classroom after school. Her attire was traditional, consisting of a dark skirt of the proper length, a high-collared white blouse, and heels. The once brown hair, now somewhat gray, was pulled back in a bun and revealed a pretty, thoughtful face.

"I just can't decide. I know I want history, but beyond that I've hit this roadblock."

"I think you know what I recommend. Apply to one or two reach schools, about five or six places you have a good shot at getting into, and one safety school that you are sure to get in–with the proviso that you love your safety school because you may end up there."

Sarah digressed a bit and asked Ms. Smith what she thought of her friends' choices.

"Those are all wonderful schools with strong history departments. It's a little different than what I suggest because besides Michigan and Illinois, which will likely admit them, they are all reach schools. But they each have two strong safe or nearly safe schools and if you apply to a fair number of reach schools, even if each of them is a long shot, you have a decent chance of getting into at least one. For example, if you apply to six reaches and the probability of getting rejected at each is ninety percent, even this old historian can do the math on that. The probability of being rejected by all six is .90 to the sixth power, which is," she said, hitting a few buttons on her calculator, "only .53."

Sarah felt a bit relieved that Ms. Smith approved of her friends' plans.

"Let's get back to you, Sarah," her teacher said. "Of all the fine schools out there, you need to narrow it down to a set to apply to, including a safety."

"The last part is easy. Illinois is my safety school."

"With your record, assuming you stay at this pace, you'll almost certainly get accepted there. Your grades are really good, and you have two papers published in *Interpretations*, with hopefully more to come." Ms. Smith was proud of the school's history journal.

"But how do I decide among the others?" Sarah asked, scratching her head.

"Well, Sarah, only you can make that choice. Why don't you see Mrs. K to get more information?"

Mrs. K, formally known as Mrs. Kawasaki, was her guidance counselor.

"Good idea."

Sarah's appointment with Mrs. K was a few days later.

"Mrs. K, I need information about universities and history programs. I've got to pick a set of schools to apply to."

"Have you talked to Ms. Smith about history programs?"

"Yes, but she said I should see you at this point."

"There are guidebooks with information about student life, academic programs, campus atmosphere, and anything else you might want to know. They range from the very serious to the lighthearted. There is also the Web site of each school."

"So I should get the books and do some research?"

"Yes, Sarah. Get back to me if you need more information."

A stop at Border's left Sarah somewhat poorer but with a stack of guidebooks. She spent the better part of a weekend in June of her junior year leafing through those and checking out schools on the Web. Once again she felt like her head was going to explode.

That Sunday afternoon their dog Fluffy was scratching at her door. Sarah ignored her. Fluffy responded by whining and then barking.

"Quiet, you dumbass dog," Sarah snapped uncharacteristically as she opened the door.

Kevin, who was walking by, asked her, "If Fluffy is a dumbass dog when she makes too much noise, does that mean that when I make too much noise I'm a dumbass human?"

"You're always a dumbass human," Sarah shot back.

Kevin, hurt by her answer, retreated to his room. A few hours later, Sarah went downstairs to find her mother, who was sitting in the study reading a magazine.

"Can I talk to you, Mom?" Sarah asked.

"Sure. I heard you snapped at Kevin. Are you stressed out by all this college stuff?"

"Yes, really stressed. I'll apologize to Kevin and take him out for ice cream later."

"That's appropriate because he's not the problem here."

"I know. But I can't make up my mind, and talking to people in the family doesn't help. All I get is conflicting advice that, when put together, equals almost every school I've ever heard of."

"Sarah, your dad and I can't make this decision for you. But at this point you should talk to him about the financial support we'll give you," her mother continued.

"Ben mentioned that to me once, but I don't think I really paid attention to all the specifics. I'll catch Dad later."

That night, after Sarah and Kevin came back with ice cream, she found her father in the study. He was reading the Sunday paper, with his feet up in one of the easy chairs.

"Dad, Mom said I should talk to you about how college will be paid for."

Her father motioned for her to sit down.

"Let me tell you how we're helping Ben, which applies to you and Kevin, too. Ben knew that he would receive $25,000 from us his first year in college, regardless of where he went. If it cost more than $25,000, he had to make up the difference from his savings, through loans or by working. If it cost less than that, he could keep the difference. Each year that goes up by five percent. So next year he gets $26,250. His third year, which is your first year, you each get around $27,500."

"What about scholarship money?" Sarah asked.

"Scholarships don't affect what you get from us. As you know, Ben received money from several different sources. That plus what he gets from the family almost covers his tuition, so he has to pay for room, board, and buy his books."

"That's an interesting plan, Dad. How did you and Mom come up with that? This is not a criticism, but I think a lot of parents pay for whatever school their kid goes to."

"It's like this; your mother and I realize, of course, that it's very expensive and we want to help. Without money from us you'd be saddled with a lot of debt. But if we give you a blank check you have no incentive to choose a less expensive place that is almost as good as your first choice. Or to go to a better and less expensive one that might not be as much fun as your first choice."

He could see that Sarah was getting a bit confused.

"I'll give you an example; one family who lives in the area, and who will remain nameless, agreed to pay for their son's education. He picked Wisconsin because he wanted to go outside of Illinois. Most likely he'd heard that the parties were better in Madison. It's not a better school than Illinois in general and actually is not as highly regarded in his major. So they ended up paying out of state tuition, which is a lot higher than tuition at a state university in Illinois. That's someone, in my opinion, passing up a better and less expensive university because it's not as much fun. I would say his decision was about vacation as opposed to education. Another family in the area who committed to pay the total cost of college had a son who went to an Ivy League school," her father continued. "Now this boy was bright, but based on who he was and his major, he was probably not going to get much more out of that school than Illinois or some of the less expensive private schools. But he had no reason to think about the costs, because he did not get any of the money that would have been saved if he had gone somewhere else. If his parents had done what we've done, he might have chosen differently."

"That makes sense, Dad."

"Now, there's obviously more to it than this. Some kids might prefer a place with smaller class sizes because they learn better in that environment, which usually means a private school. Other kids might have a major that is not so strong at the public schools in their state. Or kids who are really at the very top might not be fully challenged unless they are at a place with lots of smart students and great course offerings. But your mother and I feel that this arrangement makes each of you think carefully about the choice. You know I like analogies. It's like us paying for any new car you pick versus you paying a significant part of the price. In the first case, you'll probably buy a Maserati. In the second case, you're going to be more economical about your choice."

"Dad, I fully understand. Now I know what college will cost me. Thank God I don't have to pay the whole thing. That could be around $200,000."

"Good. Also, don't take any of what I said the wrong way. I don't mean to be critical of other parents. It's their money, and they can spend it any way they want to. It just does not make sense to me, or your mother, to sign a blank check."

"Don't worry. You know I would never say anything to anyone else."

Even though she did not call any more of her relatives to ask for advice on college choices, they continued to call her over the summer to offer it. The neighbors were also not shy about sharing their opinions with her when they saw her on the street. Sarah was as confused as ever by the multitude of choices. She felt like she was being forced to stand in front of an avalanche to get a mere handful of snow.

6
THE PLAN

At the start of her senior year, Sarah still had not made a single visit to a college campus. But after thinking about where to apply all summer, she came up with a plan that maximized the probability that she would get accepted by a top university. Plus, she was sure it would make everyone happy. When family and friends asked her where she was going, it might not be the place they'd recommended, but she was confident that they would all say, "Sarah is at a fine university."

On the first day of the fall semester, August 26, her brother Ben sent her an e-mail:

> *Dearest Sarah:*
> *I just spoke to Mom and Dad about you. Were you planning on making any campus visits or applying to any universities before you graduate from high school?*
> *Sincerely,*
> *Ben*

She quickly wrote back:

> *Dearest Ben:*
> *While I'm still not able to answer you first question, I can tell you that I'm having so much trouble deciding where I want to go to college that I'm going to apply to every four-year university in the United States.*
> *Lovingly,*
> *Your sister,*
> *Sarah*

A minute later her cell phone rang. When she pulled it from her purse, she saw that Ben was calling long distance.

"Hey, Sarah, I didn't see a smiley face at the end of your email. When you're joking you're supposed to put one in there so people don't think that you're serious. Or has Rob Taylor hacked into your computer so he can send emails pretending to come from you?"

"The email was from me and I'm not joking, Ben. I'm going to apply to all of them."

"Are you completely crazy?" Ben demanded. "That's got to be way over one thousand schools. Why would you do that?"

"Because it will get me in *The Guinness Book of World Records*?" she shot back.

"Oh, my God, be serious. Personally I think waiting this long to taper the process down is not a smart move and you're talking about not narrowing it at all."

"Well, Benjamin, it's like this; there are so many fine schools out there, and I've had so many different recommendations about where to apply that I just can't decide. So I won't. It will certainly make all our relatives and neighbors happy because I'll apply to all the schools they recommended to me. Also, the more schools I apply to, the more I'll get into by sheer chance. That's something that dawned on me after I had a talk with Ms. Smith last year. After all, Ben, it's just an application of the binomial theorem."

In Cambridge, Massachusetts, Ben Jennings slammed the palm of his hand against his head, regretting ever having rushed home in ecstasy from school one day a few years ago to show his sister Newton's binomial theorem.

"Sarah, you've gone totally nuts! I'm calling Mom and Dad to have you committed."

"What's nuts about it, Ben?"

"People usually only apply to schools they've learned more about by visiting the campus. You can't visit that many schools. You don't have the time or money."

"I've already thought of that. Other people, including you, my dear older brother, have told me that they learned very little during campus visits. They are mainly marketing sessions and the real information comes from talking to other students and reading the guidebooks. So I won't visit a single one. Besides it wouldn't be fair to the others if I see just a few out of so many deserving universities."

"Sarah, you can't go to college without ever having set foot on one."

"Oh yes I can, Ben. You just watch me."

"OK, how are you going to apply to that many schools?" Ben asked, changing to a tack on which he felt he had a better chance of winning.

"A lot of them use the Common App. That will simplify the process."

"Sarah," Ben said raising his voice. "Each school still has its own essays, so it's not just one application sent to umpteen places with the click of a button. Also, you have to pay an application fee to each school. That's a fortune."

"I'm still working on those little details, but I'm sure they're solvable," she said with an air of boredom.

"Sarah, if this is that screwball Rob Taylor's idea, I will personally come back there on the next plane and strangle him. This is not a big joke. While I agree that some people are totally overboard about all this college stuff, you still have to take it seriously."

"I *am* taking it seriously. What could be more serious than trying to get into as many universities as possible to make sure that I find the right one for me? If college is so important, then I'm actually taking this much more seriously than someone who only applies to 10 or 12 schools."

After he hung up, Ben put in a frantic call to his mother.

"Mom. Hi, it's Ben. I just wanted to inform you that your daughter is absolutely nuts."

"What do you mean?"

"I just talked to her by e-mail and then by phone, to see if she's gotten moving yet on her college applications. Do you know what she told me? She says she's going to apply to every four-year school in the country. This must be one of Rob Taylor's ideas."

"Ben, don't jump to conclusions. First, she may just be pulling your leg. Second, you don't know that Rob had anything to do with it."

"Mom, will you talk to her and see what's going on here? She sounded completely serious to me. First she waits forever to get going on this and then she goes totally overboard."

"Ben, your father is out of town on a business trip. When he gets back, he and I will talk to Sarah and I'll let you know what's up."

"OK."

The whole thing was certainly not Rob Taylor's idea, as Ben would have discovered immediately if he sat in on the session Carrie, Rob, and Sarah had the next day. Sarah informed her friends of her plan and the conversation with Ben.

"He's right, Sarah," Rob advised. "It has to be over one thousand places when you count them all, from the biggies to small liberal arts colleges and institutions backed by various religious denominations. Even absent campus visits, you can't apply to them *all*. That's over $75,000 in fees and other expenses, not to mention the work involved."

"Sarah, this is crazy. Listen to your brother and Rob," Carrie begged.

Sarah said nothing.

"This is a joke, isn't it?" Rob asked.

"No, it's not, Rob. The only thing that's a joke here is that all these people keep telling me where to go and make this such a life-or-death decision, without even asking me what I would like to study, much less what else I want."

Sarah swallowed hard.

"Since I can't decide, and it increases my chances of getting into more good schools, this is what I'm going to do," she continued.

"You really can't apply to all of them, as much as you might like to," Carrie reasoned with her in a soft voice.

Sarah thought for a few minutes.

"I understand that and I have come up with a simple solution. Instead of literally every four-year school, I'm going to apply to the top one hundred undergraduate institutions in the country, as listed by whoever has taken it upon themselves to arbitrarily rank universities. That's manageable, I think, since I'm not going to make campus visits."

"Honestly, it's more manageable," Rob concluded. "But there's still a lot of paperwork that you have to do—and the application fees."

"But the ones on the Common App are easier to finish. Sure, they have their own essays, but some of those can be reworked for a lot of different places—especially in the age of computer word processing."

"Sarah," Carrie said, shaking her head, "this is still a ton of work."

"I've thought about that, and it's not all bad. In the process I'm going to set a record that will likely stand for years. I doubt if anyone has ever applied to this many schools before."

"Who cares about records?"

"I do. Do you guys know what it's like being Ben Jennings's younger sister, given all the things he's achieved? Everyone at the high school knows him. My first two years there I was continually recruited for math team and told that I should be entering national math competitions. Since he's been at Harvard, the teachers all ask me how he's doing and say to tell him 'hello.' I don't have my own identity; I'm just Ben Jennings's sister."

Sarah saw her mother walk past the open door of her room with some folded towels, seemingly lost in her own thoughts.

"Come on. Ben doesn't lord that over you, does he?"

"No, he's cool about it. But every time I walk into his room, there it is. There are trophies on the dresser and the bookcase. Medals from math and science competitions are hanging from ribbons on the doorknobs and the curtain rods. The plaques are on the bookcase and the smaller medals and awards are in the desk drawers and in numerous boxes in the closet. His room is like a trophy case." She paused a moment. "Ben's accomplished all these great things. This will be my great achievement."

"Sarah, if you want to do this," Carrie said evenly, "we can certainly help you. My campus visits are almost all done, and I know where I'm applying, so beyond doing my own apps I have some time."

"Ladies, I'm pleased to announce that all my applications, as per the Rob Taylor Master Plan, are completed and ready to be submitted. I am–or was until Sarah came up with this idea–planning on enjoying my senior year. I have lots of time it seems and if you write your essays and such, I, along with Carrie, as needed, can certainly proofread everything before you finalize it."

"That's great, you guys. Thanks so much," Sarah gushed.

"Hey, 'All for One,'" Carrie said before Rob could get the words out.

"There's still the money side of it. It could come to almost $7,500 without postage and supplies," Rob, ever the practical one, reminded her.

"I'll tell each school that I'm applying to over one hundred places and ask them if they will waive their fee by returning the check accompanying the application. Maybe they will look at me as a student with limited financial means, based on what I'm doing. Otherwise it will come out of my savings because I don't think my parents should pay for this."

"I have another idea. We'll set up a PayPal account for you. Once the word gets out about what you're doing, we'll let people know that they can send you small amounts of money if they want to help the Sarah Jennings Application Fund. It's crazy enough that it just might work," Rob offered.

"You said a minute ago that you were applying to over one hundred schools. But before that it was one hundred. I think you need to set this in stone. I'm not going to commit to help you with this if it's open-ended and gets to be much more than one hundred."

"It's one hundred and one, Carrie. The other school is my safety school, Illinois. So technically I will be applying to the one hundred schools at the top of the list, other than Illinois, and also Illinois."

"Good choice."

"All right, how do we proceed?" Rob inquired. "I suggest we start as soon as possible and establish base camp here. You have a desk top and I can bring my laptop. That should give us all the computing and Internet access we need because you have a wireless network in the house, right?"

Sarah nodded.

"Sarah, you're responsible for paper and supplies and for doing the first drafts. Carrie and I will proofread and give you help on content. We can talk about who you should apply to first at the next meeting. We need to get going on this right away if you're going to make the deadlines at all these places."

They agreed to meet that Saturday to get started.

Later in the evening Sarah's mother pulled her aside after Kevin had gone to bed.

"Honey, Ben called me the other day. He's very worried about you. What's going on with colleges?"

"Well, Mom, I'm going to apply to the top one hundred schools in the country, plus the University of Illinois." She laid out her reasons but said nothing about the pressures she felt being Ben's sister.

"I'm going to have to talk with your father about this. I'm not sure you know what you're getting yourself into."

"Carrie and Rob have offered to help me."

"Your father will be back tomorrow. Let me talk with him before you start on this."

When John Jennings returned the next afternoon, his wife met him on the front porch. "John, we need to talk as soon as you get in the door."

"OK, I'm through the door," he said, crossing the threshold. When he put his bags down, Kate Jennings pulled him by the hand into the living room.

"It's about Sarah. She's decided to apply to quite a few schools."

"Ten?"

"Higher."

"Twenty?"

"Much higher."

"Fifty?"

"A lot higher."

"One hundred!?"

"That's about right. One hundred and one."

"What in God's name for?"

Kate Jennings outlined Sarah's reasoning to him.

"But still, this is insane," said John.

"John, when she was talking to Carrie and Rob the other day with the door open, I overheard part of their conversation. Do you know how hard it is for Sarah to be Ben's younger sister? On top of that she's the classic middle child. She's quiet but also feels lost in the shuffle."

"Ben's success shouldn't be an issue for her. He's never been anything but kind to her."

"Yes, I know. But still, she's a bit awed by what he's accomplished–and he did a lot while still in high school–and by doing this she will, in her own way, achieve something no one else has."

"Kate, I'm really against this."

"You know, John, she's your daughter."

"What??"

"I was just thinking of the story your father likes to tell about when you were in junior high and started collecting beer bottles from pre-Prohibition breweries–the story about how you were looking for this old bottle from the Schoen-something brewery because your life would not be complete unless you found one."

"It was the Schoenhofen brewery. The bottle was from before 1870 and was extremely rare."

"You biked to all the antique stores for miles around and then made him drive to dozens more until you finally found one."

"That was the Holy Grail of beer bottles. No one else, even guys who collected for decades, had ever seen one, much less owned one. In fact, the guy with the finest collection of Chicago beer bottles offered me $250 for it at the time."

"This is just as important to her. It's her Holy Grail." She paused briefly. "John, we've set boundaries for our children, and as long as they stayed inside the lines, they were allowed to be themselves. At a certain age, they could play anywhere on this block if they didn't cross the street or go around the corner and we knew where they were. As time went on, the perimeter got larger, but the rules were the same. Be home at a certain time, get your work done, and don't get in trouble, but otherwise you can be with your friends."

"I know that, but do you understand how much work this really is? And how many financial aid forms I'll have to submit?"

"Sarah said that if you fill out the appropriate ones out, beyond the standard ones like FAFSA and CSS, she'll make sure they get copied and mailed to the right schools. Plus, that comes after the application deadlines."

"I still don't like it, Kate."

"John, I think you're being inconsistent here. You can't be Adam Smith and Karl Marx at the same time."

"What the heck does that mean? What in God's name are you talking about?"

"You're the M.B.A. in the family. You came up with our financial support plan for college–giving the kids so much each year and letting them choose where they go. We've priced it out to them, as the economists say, straight out of Adam Smith. But now you want to be Karl Marx and centrally plan which schools she can apply to. If we're going to be consistent, we can't do both."

He frowned at her logic. John Jennings paused for a minute before finally conceding.

"I get what you're saying."

"Also, do you remember when Ben was a freshman and wanted to go to that summer math program on the West Coast? That was slightly unusual for a high school kid, wasn't it? But we supported him in that, and look how well it turned out."

"I still think that this is beyond the Holy Grail. It's virtually impossible. She'll never finish this along with her schoolwork."

"That may be exactly what happens. After a few weeks, she might find that it's a completely unrealistic goal. But I think we need to let her try."

"All right, fine. But she needs to know that we have the right to revisit this. If she falls behind in school or looks to be in trouble, she'll have to stop," John Jennings's voice rose as he finished the sentence.

"Agreed. I'll let her know that we talked about this and I'll call Ben to fill him in."

7
THE APPLICATION PROCESS (PART I)

After getting the green light from her parents, Sarah scheduled another appointment with Mrs. K that Friday.

"It's been a while, Sarah," Mrs. K. began. "You know that a lot of students have already made their campus visits and decided on their short lists. How about you?"

"I've decided to solve the problem by basically applying everywhere."

"Everywhere? What do you mean everywhere?"

Sarah explained about the Top 100 plus Illinois.

"This is highly unorthodox. I understand how hard this is and your concerns about getting in somewhere really good." Mrs. K was truly sympathetic. "Certainly I don't want you to end up like a girl we had a few years ago, who had her heart set on five reach schools and did not have a safety school. She did not get in to any of them and had to take some time off to apply to a more realistic set of colleges."

Mrs. K stopped for air.

"But one hundred and one? I think one student applied to fifteen places a few years ago. That seems to be the local record. I've never heard of anything more than that anywhere else, either."

Mrs. K paused again.

"Are you sure you want to do this?"

Sarah said she was and explained that her friends would help.

Full of concern, Mrs. K called Ms. Smith after Sarah left to see what she knew about this.

Sarah, Carrie, and Rob met at length that Saturday. Sarah settled on the *U. S. News and World Report* list of top undergraduate universities in the United States as the definitive list, after deciding not to bring foreign institutions into the mix. The top 100 included Illinois at number 40, so she took the top 101, which worked out nicely because six schools were tied at number 96. To estimate how long it would take to apply to 101 schools, Sarah started with the ten highest ranked schools: Harvard, Princeton, Yale, MIT, Stanford, Cal Tech, Penn, Columbia, Duke, and Chicago. They downloaded the application forms, including the Common App, and the essay questions for all ten. Because most universities, especially the most selective ones, had their regular admission deadlines around January 1, Sarah decided that it would be best for her to simply apply to them in rank order and hope that she met all the deadlines.

News of her plan spread quickly through the Oak Stream student body, as only high school rumors can. Ms. Smith called her in to chat early the next week.

"Is what I hear true, Sarah, about the number of schools you're applying to?" she asked.

"Yes, Ms. Smith, it is."

"This is highly unusual. I believe Mrs. K told you about the local record. There is a reason no one has done more. It's not effective in general, in terms of realistically changing the opportunities you have. It's also not cost-effective." Ms. Smith paused briefly and looked her straight in the eye. "Are you still determined to go ahead with this?"

"Yes, I am."

"Sarah, I urge you to *very* carefully reflect on this before you start."

"Ms. Smith, I want to do this."

Ms. Smith had a response on the tip of her tongue but decided against arguing with Sarah. "Then there are some things you need to consider in terms of the logistics here at the high school. There are transcripts that need to be sent and letters that must be submitted by your references. How many people inside school will you be getting letters from?"

"Just three. I was thinking of Mr. Harrison; Mr. Williams who taught AP American; and you."

"OK, I'm willing to help you, but you had better check with the others first. It's a lot of work for us. It would be best if you get us your list of schools as soon as possible and get the transcripts sent as well. Get that out of the way first. Second, I think it is only fair that I, my colleagues and the school insist that you finalize this list, absolutely and forever, by Thursday. No changes, no schools added, nothing after that . . ."

"Ms. Smith, I'm willing to commit to that. You'll have the list tomorrow. If you need more details, I will supply them as quickly as possible."

"Sarah," she said with a sigh, "there is more detail. Much more. Most schools have their own forms for each faculty member to fill out. We can attach the same recommendation letter we write for you to each school's form, but the forms still need to be filled in. You will have to get us those forms. How do you plan to do that?"

"I'll get you the list of schools first. Then I can bring you the forms in batches. That staggers it out rather than me bringing them all at once. Would you be willing to write a reference letter to all one hundred and one schools, Ms. Smith, while I spread the rest evenly across Mr. Harrison and Mr. Williams, if they're willing? I know that's a lot to ask, but I'd be really grateful."

Ms. Smith agreed but reminded Sarah that she should not drag the process out too long.

Various students asked Carrie and Rob if the rumor about Sarah was true. They indicated that it was and mentioned her PayPal account if anyone wanted to help financially. Sarah had been quite generous with her time in the past, helping numerous students in the library as well as dropping in on their study groups. In gratitude, seniors and juniors along with underclassmen sent her money. As the word spread, people off at college, whom she had helped in the past, PayPaled her money. The money tended to be donated in small amounts, mostly less than $15 per sender, but it added up.

Many of the relatives and neighbors who had pestered her about college sent small amounts, often in greeting cards with little jokes written inside, such as, "Here's $25. Be sure to apply to Northwestern." It was $20 here, $30 there, but after a while it added up. Her Uncle Joe, who had no children with Aunt Stephanie because "they took up so much of one's time," sent her $1000 because she was applying to so many Ivy League schools. Her godfather, Uncle Bob, sent her five years' worth of birthday checks in advance, and her parents advanced her some birthday and Christmas money. Grandma Mary, perhaps after consultation with the Pope, said she would pay the application fee for every Catholic university on the list.

As the story got around, Sarah received a phone call at home one night from Page Brooks, the editor of the student newspaper. The current staff of the *Oak Stream Sentinel* was an odd bunch who took their lead from their queen bee, Page. They were quick to offend readers, and in her editorials last year Page had criticized anyone and anything in a condescending fashion. Things had come to a head over a seemingly minor issue. A freshman had written a letter to the editor suggesting that the staff refrain from using profanity in their articles because, after all, the *Chicago Tribune* and the *New York Times* did not use such words. He had received a mocking response from Page and was attacked in print by other staffers over the next few weeks.

Carrie, Rob, and Sarah wrote letters in the freshman's defense, pointing out that he was in fact correct, and suggested that the paper should examine its editorial policies. They were attacked by the tight little clique running the *Sentinel* in an editorial response to their letters. They also received some private e-mails from the same people, mocking them for defending a freshman when they themselves were upperclassmen. What Page Brooks and her friends did not anticipate was the fire storm they set off with their condescension. Most weeks the paper was lucky to get one letter to the editor; however, the next week it had received dozens of outraged letters from students who were tired of what the *Sentinel* had become and who unanimously sided with the freshman (and, by extension, Carrie, Rob, and Sarah). Before the staff could respond in print in their usual fashion, the faculty advisor forced Page to write an apologetic editorial stating the *Sentinel*'s new standards for content and its editorial policy. Page had never been particularly close to Sarah, due to an argument they had in middle school, and now no longer acknowledged her even though they were in several classes together.

"Sarah? Oh, hello. It's Page Brooks."

"Hey, Page. How are you?" Sarah replied, looking at the receiver in surprise.

"I'm good. How are you?"

"Busy," Sarah said curtly.

"Yes, I heard about how many schools you're applying to. That's why I'm calling. I'd like to ask you about this and do a story in the *Sentinel*. Is that OK with you?"

"Sure, I guess so."

Page seemed excited that Sarah was willing to cooperate on what she thought was a fascinating feature story.

It ran the next week under the title "The Girl Who Applied Everywhere." The first few paragraphs read:

At a school like Oak Stream, where many students go on to a four-year university, a number of us have a common bond—the dreaded college application process. The information gathering, test taking, essay writing, and uncertainty about which schools will admit us is time consuming and emotionally draining. If you ever reach the point where you think you can't stand it any more, think how senior Sarah Jennings feels. She's applying to 101 different colleges.

Most students, even those in the top one percent academically, apply to ten places or less. Occasionally someone will apply to a greater number but never, based on inquiries by this writer, more than 15. So in that sense Sarah Jennings is really out there.

The Sentinel contacted the Guinness Book of World Records, and they currently do not have a category for most universities applied to or admitted to by a high school student. Based on our phone calls, they are adding those categories, and if she continues on her chosen course, Ms. Sarah Jennings will apparently hold a record or two.

The article went on to quote Sarah several times and discuss her reasons for applying to so many different institutions. Page had also interviewed Sarah's counselor, some Oak Stream faculty members, and admissions officers at local universities. The story closed with a mention of Sarah's PayPal address and promised to keep the readers informed on her progress.

The *Chicago Sun-Times*, the more tabloid like of Chicago's two daily newspapers, did a story of its own on Sarah. After putting out a query to other newspapers, they reported that a football player in California once applied to 30 four-year universities. Intent on receiving a full scholarship to play at the college level, he had applied to every school in the California state college system, some of the smaller ones in the University of California system, and a few universities in neighboring states. His efforts had been rewarded with a free ride to Cal Poly.

The *Sun-Times* also interviewed Rob Taylor, described as Sarah's helper in the process, who elicited donations to cover her expenses. A few days after the article ran, her PayPal account swelled to more than half the amount needed for application fees and supplies. These funds, along with the money from other sources, covered the lion's share of her expenses.

Sarah also became a conversation piece at Oak Stream. The student body was large, as high schools go, with 800 in the senior class, so it was impossible to know everyone. But, frequently, as she walked down the halls, students pointed or motioned with their heads and told their friends that the blonde who just went by was the "Girl Who Applied Everywhere."

Returning to school after the summer break, taking various AP classes, and getting back into the intensive training of cross-country were demanding enough. Beyond that, during the next two weeks Sarah spent all her spare moments on the applications.

As a first step, at Mrs. K's suggestion, Sarah drafted a very general essay about who she was, what she enjoyed, what she wanted to do with her life, and how college fit in with her plans. Rob, who was just a phone call away most nights, came over one Wednesday after Sarah had revised the draft several times.

"It won't do as is," he said sternly after reading it twice.

"What's the problem?" Sarah asked, a little defensively.

"I'd say that in terms of being deeply introspective and reflective, it's great. It talks about things most people won't know about you, including things I didn't realize, and I've been your friend as long as anyone. But you have to remember that any essay you write for a college application is a marketing tool. You are convincing Insert College Name Here that they should choose you rather than the hundreds of other applicants who look just like you on paper."

He paused for a moment, trying to see if he had been too harsh with

Sarah.

"Take this paragraph here. You talk about how well you get along with others, help them whenever possible, and how hurt you are when people don't like you. On a college application that sounds like you're a bit dependent emotionally. You don't want to convey that in an essay. I think you can say the same thing in a much more positive way. Make this an asset they get if they admit Sarah Jennings. Not only is she smart and everything they want in terms of her as an individual, but she helps others. Any dorm you're in, team or group you're on, class you're in, you'll help other people because that's what you do."

"Actually, I have helped people at Oak Stream with things," she offered in return, seeing the point Rob was trying to make.

"*Helped people*? Sarah, you're the Michael Jordan of Oak Stream High School. Beyond your own academic strengths as an individual, you make everyone around you better, just as Michael Jordan did with the Bulls," he said frankly. "Obviously, you can't say it that way in the application because it would sound too arrogant. But they want self-confidence and some indication that you're not self-centered—that there's some deeper substance to the applicant than just standardized test scores and grades."

"I get it, Rob."

"And you do have it, Sarah. Not like the kids who have this essentially fake community service stuff in their background, just to dress up their applications. Where Mom and Dad shell out $9,000 so they can go to Central America for eight weeks and help build a community center in a place they don't care about and will never think about again. Or the stories you hear about kids who are heavy coke users at weekend parties but do volunteer work preaching against drug use as if they've never tried the stuff in their lives. I heard that colleges are starting to see through all this." Rob paused again to catch his breath. "Sarah, you help people every time they ask you, and none of it is for show because it's all behind the scenes. But you can talk about it in this type of essay, if it fits their application requirements, to let them know about it."

Sarah tackled the essays from the top ten schools next. Since Harvard was using the Common App, its essay topics were the same. The Common App allowed people to write on one of five topics or a topic of the student's own choice. Scanning the list, she decided quickly that there was no really significant experience in her life, issue of local, national, or international concern or actual person who had influenced her sufficiently for Sarah to write about (and she wondered how many high school students felt the same way). She was also a bit stuck on what to write about regarding diversity in society. That left either the topic of her choice or the question about how a fictional or historical figure had influenced her. Unlike her brother Ben, who had used his essay for Chicago on which mathematical function best described him as his essay of choice for the Common App, she shied away from picking her own topic. Sarah finally settled on D'Artagnan, the hero in *The Three Musketeers*, as the character who had most influenced her.

Her essay read:

I have been greatly influenced by the character D'Artagnan (whose story closely follows in important ways that of the real life D'Artagnan, Charles de Batz-Castelmore) introduced in the The Three Musketeers by Alexandre Dumas. As many young Gascons did before him, in the novel he came to Paris to seek his fortune. He was of humble origin and brought with him, beyond a letter of introduction from his father to Monsieur de Treville (the captain of the king's musketeers), only a sword, a broken-down old horse, a small sum of money, and his father's sound advice. With great spirit he quickly befriended three of the king's musketeers—Athos, Porthos, and Aramis—and even though he was unfamiliar with politics at the court, his innate sense of right and wrong led him to take their side against the cardinal's guards and eventually Cardinal Richelieu himself. D'Artagnan defended the honor of the queen as well as that of France and in the process became an officer of the musketeer regiment by the end of the book, eventually achieving a fair degree of fame and fortune. Just as the real-life D'Artagnan became a confidante of kings and was rewarded by them for his loyal service.

D'Artagnan has influenced me by illustrating what can be achieved by someone, even though he is young and without wealth or connections, but has the right attributes in terms of his or her character. Surely if he could accomplish so much in the rigid class system of seventeenth-century France, a teenager in our upwardly mobile society with a proper secondary school education and a good work ethic has almost unlimited opportunities in front of her. While Dumas's novel is most commonly interpreted as an epic swashbuckler full of courage, cunning, and bravado, I regard it equally as a seventeenth-century Horatio Alger story. It indicates that the opportunities are great if one is willing to aim high and not deviate from those goals. D'Artagnan has also shown me the importance of loyalty and courage, even in the face of great odds. Much of what he accomplished was because he stood up and stood by his friends, and they by him, as they continually faced adversity.

As I am about to start on my own (academic) journey away from my home and family to study history at a top university, I see a number of parallels between D'Artagnan and me. I come from a fairly average background and bring with me "only" a solid high school education, a strong sense of right and wrong instilled in me by my family, a willingness to work hard, and a loyalty to my friends, which leads me to help others, should they only ask. But I hope to achieve many things: not just a bachelor's degree in history, but after that an advanced degree or degrees in history, law, or business administration, which will prepare me for a career in teaching and possibly research, the legal world, or in business. In the process, the students at the university I attend while an undergraduate will be my Athos, Porthos, and Aramis as we work together to reach our goals, and the faculty, staff, and administration will play the role of Monsieur de Treville, counseling me and guiding me along the way.[2]

Happy with herself for completing the first essay, she sent it by e-mail to Carrie and Rob who were doing their homework. Rob responded first, to Sarah only.

> *Sarah:*
> *Initially I was a bit put off by the fact that you are referring to a "fictional" character, especially D'Artagnan, because The Three Musketeers is often viewed as a book written for children.*
> *But you make it clear that you know the underlying history, that D'Artagnan was a real individual, and that there are deeper lessons in the book than in a simple adventure story. As a history student (and you're telling them that you'll be a history major), I think it's quite acceptable for you to refer to historical fiction, especially because the "One for All and All for One" motto of the principal characters lets you talk about your own team spirit and loyalty to friends.*
> *Nice essay!*
> *Rob*

Carrie responded a few minutes later, by hitting the "Reply All" button.

> *Sarah:*
> *I'm not sure if this is the right choice here, especially because you'll be using this for all the schools on the Common App. This book is seen as a kid's story and it may strike the admissions people reading it as sort of (forgive me for saying this) childish. Although your essay is well written, in my opinion.*
> *Carrie*

Rob, who was in the loop on Carrie's e-mail, responded before Sarah could reply.

> *Carrie:*
> *I understand what you're trying to say and I partly had the same reaction at first. But I don't agree. It's not like Sarah is talking about Batman in a comic book inspiring her. This is a great work of historical fiction, and she makes it clear (and can make it clearer) that she knows the history behind it. See, for example, the preface to the really good Penguin edition of the book, which traces the history of the real-life D'Artagnan, Athos, Porthos, Aramis, and Monsieur de Treville for the*

---

[2] The story of the real-life D'Artagnan, Monsieur de Treville and the Three Musketeers can be found, for example, in Karin Maund and Phil Manson, The Four Musketeers (Tempus Publishing, 2005).

reader.

> *Sarah draws insights from the story and explains how it parallels her own case as she is applying to schools. What if she adds some footnotes to the essay from the Penguin edition? What could be more academic-looking to a university than an essay with footnotes, especially when many of the readers probably don't know that Dumas's characters really did exist?*
> *Rob*

Although Rob could be a little long-winded when he got going, he was convincing. Carrie acquiesced and found a wonderful book in French about the history of the Dumas characters at a local university library. Sarah added it as one of several historical references in her essay, after Carrie translated the relevant passages for her.

Most of the other schools in the Top 10 required some additional work. Yale, Stanford, Duke, and Chicago were on the Common App, but, except for Duke, they all wanted at least one more essay. Yale hoped that students would write about something that was not otherwise apparent on the application. Sarah reworked the reflective essay that Mrs. K. had suggested, emphasizing her ability to help others. This was saved as Essay 2 on her computer; the one for the Common App was stored as Essay 1. Stanford wanted Sarah to not only discuss an intellectual experience she had had but also to write about why Stanford was a good place for her and to disclose something that would help her roommate know her better. Sarah wrote about her project in AP statistics analyzing data to explain why slavery thrived in certain states and not in others in the United States before the Civil War. This essay (Essay 3 on her computer) also worked for Cal Tech, which wanted discussion of her interest in math or science. For the other two Stanford essays, Sarah talked about the quality of the history faculty there and reworked her Essay 2 to meet the 250-word requirement.

Chicago, of course, was famous for its unique, quirky essay topics. Some of them were simple quotes that the applicant was asked to discuss, such as "At present you need to live the question," a line from the writings of Rainer Maria Rilke. Students could also make up their own prompt, which led Sarah to rewrite her Essay 2 based on the quote "One for All and All for One." It was saved as Essay 2.1.

Of the schools not on the Common App, Penn's questions were idiosyncratic, asking which faculty members the student would like to study with and about the student's interest in Penn in general. She stored those as Penn1 and Penn2 on her machine, in case she needed them later. Columbia asked the applicant to convey a sense of who he or she is. Sarah combined, after a good deal of dovetailing and editing, Essay 1 and Essay 2 for Columbia. MIT gave her two choices. Sarah picked their Essay B, which asked her to "Describe the world you come from, for example your family, clubs, school, community, city, or town. How has that world shaped your dreams and aspirations?" She created it by reworking her Columbia essay to stress the influence of people and institutions on her.

Princeton allowed students to use either the Common App (with a supplemental essay) or its own application, which required two essays. Sarah chose Princeton's application and used Essay 1 as her main essay, because they wanted to hear about a person she was influenced by. For the second essay, she chose "One for All and All for One" as her favorite quotation and gave them Essay 2.1.

Quite proud of herself for getting the first ten applications done, Sarah scheduled a meeting at her house with Carrie and Rob for Saturday, September 13. They proofread the applications and her essays with the critical eye that sometimes only friends can provide. Barring some minor corrections, everything was certified as ready to go.

"Woo-hoo!" she exclaimed as they ate cupcakes. "The first ten are out of the way."

"Sarah, it's good that you've finished them, but it's also not cause for great celebration. You're three weeks in, and ten are done. You have about fifteen more weeks until the end of the calendar year and ninety left to do. At this pace—ten every three weeks—you'll only complete sixty of the applications," Carrie said to her somewhat critically.

Like everyone else, Carrie was, even if deep under the surface, a product of her own, often critical, upbringing.

"That's not an accurate estimate, Carrie. I didn't even start these ten until the second week of the term, so I really did them in about ten days. Plus, what I've learned from this is that my main essays, sometimes with small changes, are reusable for many other schools. There won't be too many places with off-beat topics like Chicago."

"True, but this is the start of the semester. Classes aren't really intense yet. You'll need time—no matter how well you plan in advance—for term papers, homework, and projects. Also, you're on a bit of an adrenalin rush right now. Attacking the first ten apps, to the top places, has probably even been fun," Rob said in almost a parental tone. "But you'll hit a wall eventually somewhere during the process. It won't get easier."

"Other things will change in my favor, though, as time goes on. The regional meet is in late October. We may not qualify for the sectionals as a team. I most likely won't make it as an individual runner either, so the season should be over at that point. Then there's Christmas break."

"Winter break doesn't start until December twenty-second, so you don't have a ton of time there. I also think that the end of cross-country will be a welcome relief that will not make you want to jump deeper into the application process," Carrie stated. Her comments were based on past observation of Sarah's fall schedule. "You've got to pick up the pace here,

Sarah, if for no other reason than you need a cushion for unforeseen events. What if you catch the flu or something?"

"I agree," Rob added. "I think you should, as another test of the process, try and do the next twenty applications in two weeks. I realize it's unreasonable to expect you to finish them all, but let's see how many you can have for us to look at on Saturday, September twenty-seventh."

"That's good, Rob," Carrie responded before Sarah could say anything. "At that point we'll know a lot more about the process."

Sarah agreed somewhat reluctantly, and they enjoyed a quiet evening sitting on her back porch looking at the stars. The next day Sarah rose early and jumped back into it, printing and organizing the paperwork for the next 20 schools. Her parents asked if they could help, but she did not want to burden them with what she saw as her own work. Beyond having them pick up more printer paper and ink cartridges, she left them out of it.

Rob was right. AP European history, which was regarded as the hardest course at Oak Stream, started to eat up more of her time. Along with the work in her other classes, many nights she felt totally spent after eating a quick dinner, taking a shower, and doing her homework. The fact that Carrie and/or Rob were usually huddled in one corner of her room doing their own schoolwork and waiting for her to give them something to read kept her mind on the applications. She would toss them an essay or form to review after finalizing it, often late at night, and they would mark it up in red pen and send it back her way. Some days they closed shop at one in the morning.

Sarah found she had little time for anything but homework and college applications. Cross-country was her only relief during those two weeks, the physical exertion taking her mind off the paperwork. She attacked the miles with sheer joy and her times improved greatly, setting several personal records at the meets in the process. Her coach noted this and told her that she was an integral part of the team this year. Sarah watched none of the television shows that had been a break for her during her previous years of high school. Opportunities to go out for ice cream with her family evaporated, and there was little time for IM-ing, texting, or idle chatter via e-mail. A baseball fan, but always joyfully agnostic regarding Chicago's two major league teams, she missed the golden opportunity of seeing them both make a successful run to the play-offs during September 2008. The silver lining on this cloud was that she did not watch a single play-off game on television and was spared seeing the Cubs and White Sox both crash out of the play-offs in early October.

Sarah also was totally absent for the heart of her first real presidential campaign, with local favorite Barack Obama running against John McCain. For a history major interested in public affairs, with one of the most interesting races in years unfolding before her, that was quite a lot to miss.

From September 1 onward, it all went right past her. Sarah Palin and the impersonations of her on *Saturday Night Live* were just background noise. Sarah didn't see any of the debates but in the process she also avoided watching the panel of commentators on CNN, who outnumbered the attendees at the Last Supper and dissected every word of every sentence uttered.

After a grueling couple of weeks, the trio met again in Sarah's room after dinner on September 27. Putting on the finishing touches as Carrie and Rob arrived, Sarah handed them a stack of applications. Ignoring the details, Rob quickly counted them before he spoke.

"You did fourteen more, Sarah. I'm sure they're all fine and we can deal with the proofreading in a little bit. If you continue at this rate, doing one a day on average, you will have–*bing, bing, bing*–ninety-four done on December sixth. That would get you to one hundred and one by December thirteenth. You're basically on schedule if you keep to this pace–assuming, of course, that you don't come down sick. But you've got to continue at this rate and keep the last two weeks in December as a buffer."

"I can handle it," she reassured them.

"Sarah, it's going to get harder. The historiography section of AP Euro is coming up, and that's the highest peak in the academic Himalayas at Oak Stream. I'm sure Ben has told you about it," said Rob.

The paper they were required to write on historiography was notoriously tough. Ben had been e-mailing her regularly to give her his advice about this requirement.

"I can handle it," she repeated.

"Sarah," Rob said mildly, sensing that she was getting stressed, "given the tightness of the schedule, I think you have to economize with your free time. Otherwise you're not going to make it."

"Free time? *What* free time? I don't watch TV. I've missed the baseball playoffs and weeks of the presidential campaign. I don't even know who Sarah Palin is or what Joe Biden thinks."

"Neither does anyone else. But getting back to the main point, I think you have to cut some more to keep on schedule. We'll have to skip homecoming this year, and right now I think you better tell your parents that you might be unavailable for Christmas, except for opening presents on December twenty-fifth. You need to keep that time open, so you really can't commit to any vacations or holiday parties," Rob argued with her.

Carrie glanced curiously at Rob.

Uncoupled, they had gone to the homecoming dance last year as a group of three. Connecting with nine unattached kids, including Frank Foster and Joey Merlino, they had had the time of their lives. The DJ was good, the music was hot, and they danced until the party ended. After that they went to a pizza place near school and then drove to a nearby park.

Because it was homecoming night, the police ignored them, and they joked and talked until the early morning. Several friendships in the group of 12 people were greatly strengthened that night.

"Skip homecoming? It's next Saturday. Oh, come on, we had such a good time last year. Plus, I'm really not going to miss all of the fun around Christmas."

"Sarah, look. You wanted to do this. You committed to it. We're the ones helping you. No one is saying that you can't celebrate Christmas. If the schedule holds, you will have the last half of December to relax and enjoy the holidays. But you just can't assume that. You need to tell your parents not to plan on you for much around Christmas."

Carrie nodded in agreement. For Sarah this year there would be no baking cookies or shopping trips and adventures at the mall with Carrie.

"OK. But homecoming? It's such a blast."

"I know, Sarah. But every day is vital," Carrie reminded her with a sigh of anticipated regret.

"Fine, then no homecoming this year. But I'm going to blow it out around Christmas as soon as I finish all this!"

"Sarah, we'll have our own celebration here the night of the homecoming dance. It might not be like last year, but we'll have fun nonetheless. Let's schedule the next meeting for then," Rob suggested.

They put the date on Sarah's wall calendar and turned to the final reading of her materials. After an hour they tore open the box of Hostess cupcakes Rob had brought along.

"You're almost a quarter done with this, Sarah. Congratulations," Rob told her.

With pencils held aloft in their right hands, they touched the tips together and intoned, "Cupcakes for all and all for cupcakes."

The next week was tougher; the late nights were starting to affect Sarah. In the morning, for the first time in her life, she asked her parents to make her coffee even though she hated the taste of it. At cross-country practice her times did not get better versus the previous week. The coach, who was used to her continuous improvement, looked at her with mild displeasure. But otherwise Sarah kept at it. Carrie was around less than before, as she was working on her own applications, but by the end of the week Sarah had cranked out seven more applications.

"Here you go," she said, handing them to Carrie and Rob on the night of October 4, "another batch right on schedule."

After completing the work for the evening, Rob told them he had a surprise. He excused himself and returned with a big white cardboard box.

"Cupcakes specially made by Bauer's," he said in response to their quizzical looks. Bauer's was an old-time German bakery in town, a place where little old ladies behind the counter called you "honey" and broke off the string they tied the boxes in with their bare hands. Run by the same family for generations, it was famous throughout the area for its donuts and pastries. "Extra-large cupcakes made with yellow cake and chocolate icing. No Hostess tonight. But first, I've ordered pepperoni pizza and garlic bread from Accardo's, which should be here in about thirty minutes."

"Rob, you are so great," Sarah gushed.

"Hey, I told you we're having our own homecoming party here tonight."

"Only if I can pay for part of it," Carrie demanded as she pulled some bills from her purse. Before Sarah could speak, Carrie said, "It's on us."

"Thank you, guys."

They played music from Sarah's iPod until the food arrived and talked about who was with whom at the dance. Apparently Frank Foster was going with Laurie Benton. Laurie was cute and nice but not very intellectual, which made her an odd match, in their minds, for Frank. Carrie seemed especially surprised that they were dating.

After the main course they attacked the cupcakes, inviting Kevin into the room to join them. When the food was gone, they retreated to the Jennings's backyard and burned wood in the fire pit before fatigue got them at three in the morning.

The following week was rough. Sarah caught a cold, which sapped her energy. Long distance running only made it worse, but by the team rules, she could not skip practices if she was in school. Most nights she could barely keep her eyes open after 9 p.m. Carrie was increasingly absent and it was now Rob's job to shake Sarah awake and run down to the kitchen to make her hot chocolate. Nonetheless, several nights she had to call it quits early to get some decent sleep for fear of what she would be like otherwise in the morning. By the end of the week, at the next formal meeting with her friends, Sarah had three more applications completed.

"You're at thirty-four in total now, Sarah. Puts you a bit behind where you want to be, but we can write that off to your cold." Rob was increasingly playing the role of taskmaster in her application process. "Or, to say it this way, this uses up three of your buffer days we allocated to late December. If you can complete ten to fourteen apps in the next two weeks, you'll be in good shape. Next week is a good week; we've got four days off for parent-teacher conferences and other stuff so you can really crank on it then."

"But I've got to start the research on my historiography paper," she pleaded.

"What are you writing on?" Carrie asked.

Ms. Smith had given the students a list of topics to choose from and had provided them with useful references on each one.

"I'm going to compare economic history and the use of statistical analysis of data to test historical hypotheses to the standard historical method pioneered by von Ranke."

"Oh my God! You must be freaking joking. Can't you pick something easier?" Rob asked. Rumor had it that no one had ever done this particular topic before.

"No, I want to do it. In the past no one worked on this because they hadn't finished AP economics and AP statistics by this point. Besides, I think Ms. Smith will like it if I tackle this."

"It's a ton of hard work, on top of the application process," Carrie noted in a way she hoped would convince Sarah not to choose it.

"And I won't be around much next week because I've got to get started on my own paper in AP Euro. So it's going to be up to you to keep on top of this."

"I know that, Rob," Sarah said sharply.

"All right, next formal meeting scheduled for October twenty-fifth in this very room. By that point Sarah should be almost half done," Carrie interjected.

Although they were largely off school that week, Sarah still had cross-country practice and the conference meet was coming up on Saturday. Due to the residual effects of her cold and increasing academic anxiety, Sarah's times started to actually worsen and the coach became a bit peeved with her. She was still one of the top seven so she ran with the varsity at the conference meet, but her time was lackluster. In the calculations inherent in distance running, it was clear that if she had come in her normal third among the Oak Stream runners rather than fifth, they would have finished second overall rather than fourth. She was relieved more than hurt when the coach brought up three sophomores for the regional meet and dropped Sarah from the varsity squad.

Because she was focusing on her AP Euro paper, she completed just seven applications in those two weeks.

When she met with Carrie and Rob on the 25th, they were both surprised at the low number.

"Let's take stock here, Sarah," Rob began rather stiffly. "You've now completed forty-one applications, as opposed to the fifty-two you would have completed if you'd done seven a week as you originally agreed to. If you can finish seven a week from here on out, you'll be done on Christmas Eve."

"OK, so I'll be done on Christmas Eve. Big deal."

"That's not the point. Any more slippage and you won't make it."

"Slippage? Slippage? Is that what this is? Look, I've been working my butt off and I don't need to be criticized about it," she said loudly, gesturing at the piles of paper in her room.

"Sarah, I'm not criticizing. I'm just stating the facts," Rob replied, raising his voice as well.

"I know what the facts are," she shot back. "The facts are that I'm doing the best I can."

"Hey, I'm just trying to help, like you asked us to."

"But you're not helping, Rob, by yelling at me and acting like you're Simon Cowell or something. They're my applications, not yours!"

"Yes, Sarah, they're your applications. What do you want me to do?"

"I want you to quit being such a pain in the ass!"

"Fine! If that's how you feel, you can do them by yourself. I'm out of here," Rob yelled as he shut the door.

Carrie shot her a concerned look.

"I can do this, Carrie, with or without Rob imitating Pharaoh overseeing the building of the pyramids."

"OK, let's drop the whole subject for one night. I think that would be best."

They went downstairs and watched television in the family room, something Sarah had not done in weeks. But she hardly said another word the rest of the night. Before Carrie left, she agreed to drop by as often as she could or look at drafts sent by e-mail before they met to assess her progress again on November 8.

Sarah and Rob were extremely cold to each other at school the next Monday, and he no longer came to her house or communicated with her electronically. On a positive note, an Associated Press writer in the Chicago office followed up on Sarah's story in the *Sun-Times* with his own article entitled "101 Applications." A number of newspapers around the country ran the story. It gave Sarah an adrenalin rush to learn that it appeared nationally, and she picked up steam again. Up in her room, completely alone most of the time, Sarah felt a bit lost. But she chanted softly to herself, "I can do this. I can do this."

The presidential election came and went without Sarah taking much notice. When her mother knocked softly on the door to tell her that Barack Obama had won, she responded briefly, "Tell him congratulations from me if you see him."

By Friday, November 7, she had finished another 16 applications and also made significant progress on her historiography paper. The family went to their favorite Mexican restaurant, and Sarah came back quite buoyant, eager to dispense with two or three more colleges by the time Carrie arrived the next evening. That would get her to about 60 applications completed and would recover some of the lost time.

When she turned on the machine in her room, it clicked several times, and then there was a smell of burnt something or other coming from the box. As it started to boot up, the screen went dead. She immediately shut everything off.

"Goddamn it!!" Sarah screamed at the top of her lungs.

Her mother, who happened to be walking by with a basket of folded laundry–normally a chore of Sarah's, but one that she had not touched since early September–rushed into the room.

"What happened?"

"Mom, I think my machine just fried!"

"Are you backed up?"

"Only partly. I copied the important stuff onto my memory stick on Tuesday. But I didn't back up the last version of my Historiography paper, which I just made major revisions to. And it means that I've probably lost the essays for four colleges."

"Oh, honey, it will be OK," her mother said in the reassuring tone that is a parental near monopoly.

"No, it won't. I'm totally screwed. I'm already behind on the college stuff, and the history paper will take me time to rewrite if it's lost. Plus I just don't have the energy to do it after all this!"

Sarah collapsed on the bed, her face in her hands, and burst into tears.

8
THE APPLICATION PROCESS (PART II)

Sarah's mother quickly descended the long steps from the second floor to the kitchen and picked up the phone. From memory she dialed the Taylors' number and asked for Rob.

"Rob, this is Mrs. Jennings."

"Hi, Mrs. Jennings," he answered uncertainly.

"Can you come over and help Sarah?"

"Ahhhh, Mrs. Jennings, I don't think so. We had a big fight, and we haven't talked to each other for about two weeks. She really does not want me there."

"Please, Rob, it's serious," Mrs. Jennings begged. "Sarah's having a complete meltdown. She's up in her room crying her eyes out."

"What happened?"

"She's been working like crazy this week, on her history paper and on the applications. It looks like something happened to her computer, and she may have lost a lot of work."

"I'll call Carrie, and we'll be right over." Rob grabbed his jacket from a kitchen chair and headed out the door.

After a quick walk, he waited on the Jennings's front porch until Carrie arrived. She agreed to let Rob go in first. He climbed the steps and knocked softly on the bedroom door.

"Who is it?" Sarah called plaintively.

"It's Rob. Can I come in?"

"No, go away."

"Sarah, you have to let me in," he replied, opening the door and entering the room.

She rose from the bed, her eyes moist with tears. Rob, after a growth spurt the last few years, stood two inches taller than Sarah. His Waco Brothers T-shirt was partly covered by a thin blue jacket about the same color as his jeans.

"Sarah, I'm really sorry about what happened last time I was here. I wasn't trying to be such a slave driver. I just sensed that this was very important to you, and I wanted to help. The only way I could was by reading what you wrote and keeping track of the schedule."

"Rob, I know. I'm sorry for the way that I yelled at you. This all started out as a big adventure. At least I thought it would be, with me applying to all these great places. But it's not so much fun anymore."

"I guess not," Rob said sympathetically. He handed her some tissues to dry her eyes. "Do you still want me to help?"

"Yes, if you want to."

"Sure, but only to the extent you want me to."

"Great. Let me worry about the schedule. Just give me advice."

"All right. It's completely your process, Sarah. They're your applications."

"OK," she said, giving Rob a quick hug.

Carrie knocked when she sensed that it was all right to join them.

"Hey," she said from the hallway. "Is everything OK?"

"Yes, we're good."

"Then fill me in. If there were no problems with your machine, how many apps would you have done now?" Carrie asked.

"I finished number fifty-seven on Friday afternoon."

"That's not bad."

Sarah gave them the details about her machine.

"Sarah," Carrie spoke because she felt it was better that it did not come from Rob, "from now on back every single thing up as you're working on it. It's good practice to do it every ten minutes. You really can not endure this again."

"I know. I was just flying through it all and didn't want to stop."

"You can get a tech to come out tomorrow morning if you call now. They should be able to find the problem and get back to you quickly–if you pay a rush charge. Rob can bring his laptop over, and we can work on that in the meantime. In the worst case scenario, all changes since your last backup were lost. How bad is that?"

"The worst part is the paper for Euro. I was doing the revisions at the keyboard rather than on paper so I don't have a written version of them. The four apps had essays that were pretty standard, so I just reworked my Essay 1 for those schools."

"If you go back through the last version, you can probably remember the changes to your Euro paper. It hasn't been that long. The apps lost are not that big of a deal," Carrie said, summarizing quickly. "Since you were filling out the forms online Rob can check those on his laptop if you give him your password and account information. I'll read the new essays you have printed out. That lets you concentrate on your Euro paper. I suggest you find a quiet place somewhere, go back through your last hard copy, and mark down all the changes you remember."

Sarah wanted to get out of the house, but the village library was closing any minute so she went down to the basement and reread the paper there. The next day the computer tech pronounced that her hard drive was dead. Rather than trying to retrieve what was on there through a recovery service, they wrote it off and had a new one installed. Rob, who was computer proficient, reloaded all her essential programs on the machine along with her application materials. She was up and running again by Saturday night.

Despite being emotionally drained, Sarah kept at it, knowing that she had to get the Euro paper back to where it had been before the hard drive crashed. By Sunday night she felt it was up to speed. She would gladly have collapsed at that point, but Carrie and Rob suggested she go back to the four lost applications before they faded from memory. She revisited them on Sunday night and made some quick notes about what she needed to do in terms of completing the forms and tweaking one particular essay.

"Guys, how about if we meet here Wednesday night at seven? I'll have the four 'lost' apps ready for you to check, and if I get some time, since Tuesday is Veterans Day and we're off school, maybe some more."

"Great."

On Monday morning, Sarah felt worse than she had for years. There were bags under her eyes, something she thought happened only to adults. Despite two cups of coffee with breakfast, she had trouble staying awake. Although it was against the rules, she bought the strongest coffee available in the cafeteria and brought it with her to class. A few weeks ago she had been taking it with two creams and two sugars to hide the taste. Now she drank the coffee jet-black. The teachers, knowing that she was a not a troublemaker, looked at her curiously but let the infraction go. In spite of all this, Sarah nodded off in class during seventh and eighth periods.

By Tuesday she felt a bit better, finishing the four applications that had been lost and doing one more. She started another and finished it Wednesday after school. At the appointed time her friends arrived and were apprized of the situation.

"So the number's fifty-nine now, right?" Carrie asked.

"Correct, I'm done with fifty-nine, after you guys look over these."

"What's your plan from here on out?" Rob asked.

"I'll turn in my Euro paper in a couple of days. I don't see anything else really major coming up in school before Christmas. So I'll have lots of time for applications. I plan to do one a day, on average. On that schedule

I'll have eighty done by December third, ninety-four applications done on December seventeenth, and one hundred and one finished on December twenty-fourth, Christmas Eve. Perfect."

"That's cutting it a bit close because you only have a one-week buffer zone," Carrie reminded her after glancing at Rob. "You still have to go to class and keep up with your homework. Otherwise you'll pay the price on your final exams."

"I'm not going to blow off school, Carrie, but I can coast a bit. I'll keep up with the readings and assignments but not do much more until I'm done with the college stuff. Finals don't start until January twentieth, so I've got almost three weeks in January to really study. Plus, if it gets tight, my parents have agreed to let me stay home from school on December eighteenth and nineteenth. Nothing important happens anyway, and I'll be sure to pre-arrange to get the notes from someone in the classes you guys are not in."

"You got a lot done these last two weeks, even with the computer problems. If you can keep it up, you might just make it. In the spirit of further help, I'm pleased to announce the R.E. Taylor incentive plan."

"What?" Carrie and Sarah asked. Rob, whose middle name was Edward, never referred to himself by his initials and neither did anyone else they knew.

"It's my incentive plan for Sarah. Every time you finish five applications from here on out, I will award you a $10 gift certificate to Bauer's Bakery." Sarah had an incredible sweet tooth that, some days, only Bauer's could satisfy.

"I didn't know Bauer's had gift certificates," Carrie added.

"They do now. When I told them it was for Sarah, they started it. They are doing their part, in exchange for my assurance that they are now the Official Bakery of Sarah Jennings."

Everyone laughed.

"Oh, I kind of also have another announcement," Rob added.

"Now what?"

"Sarah, the reason I was so upset with you a few weeks ago . . ."

"Rob, forget it. We don't need to go back there," Sarah said, cutting in.

"No, let me finish. It pertains to my announcement. When I thought about it later, I realized that part of the reason I was getting upset was that you were having all the fun. I was doing the grunt work, like proofreading, and then getting yelled at. So, I've decided to get in on the action. I shall be submitting nine more college applications," he said with a slight smile as he ran his hand through his brown hair.

"I thought you had already picked your schools?"

"I have, Carrie. I will be applying to the same nine schools."

"It serves no purpose to apply again. You've already applied to those places," Sarah said in complete confusion.

"Actually, that's not quite true. Robert Edward Taylor has applied to those nine places." Rob paused for a moment for effect. "I'm legally changing my name to Running Elk Taylor to get back to my Potawatomi roots. I've already started the process and I've been assured that it only takes a few more weeks. Running Elk Taylor will apply to the same nine schools, now checking off the Native American box on the applications."

Carrie and Sarah looked at each other, thinking that they had not heard correctly.

"You see, it has occurred to me," he stated philosophically, "that America's finest universities might not admit Robert Edward Taylor. Let's see if they admit Running Elk Taylor."

"So from now on your name is Running Elk? I've known you since second grade. I'm not going to start calling you Running Elk," Sarah said emphatically, gesturing at Rob with a ballpoint pen.

"You two, since you are among my oldest and dearest friends, may call me R.E.," he said with a wave of his right hand.

"Since you've gone completely frigging nuts, I'm willing to help with the process," Carrie interjected. "How about this for your extracurricular activities in the area of community service? You can say that you started out teaching courses in buffalo hunting and scalping on the reservation and then modernized the curriculum to include casino management. That ought to really impress the admissions committees."

"As a Native American I find those remarks full of prejudice and deeply offensive, Miss Wilson."

"My apologies to your Indian forefathers, Mr. Taylor," Carrie replied in the same tone.

"They're called Native Americans, not Indians, Carrie."

"Sorry."

"Rob, I mean R.E., you don't have a ton of time to do this and you said you still have lots of work to do on your Euro paper."

"It's really not a problem. I'm turning in exactly the same applications, essays and all. I have the essays all stored on my PC and I have hard copies of the application forms in my room."

Sarah was not surprised that he still had them because he never threw anything out. A few weeks ago she had found a drawing he'd made in second grade still sitting on his desk, with Mrs. Reinhart's insightful comments on it.

"The only difference will be my name and my ethnicity. I also have to submit transcripts in my new name and will ask the teachers to resubmit their letters of recommendation for Running Elk Taylor. I can get everything prepared, beyond the letters, which they can send now, so that the applications will be ready as soon as my name change comes through.

Don't worry, Sarah, I'll still have plenty of time to help you."

Carrie looked at Sarah in complete amazement, shaking her head and turning her palms up.

"I'm sure that my Indian ancestors would be quite proud of me, Carrie."

"Indians, R.E.? They were Native Americans a minute ago," Carrie threw back at him.

He scowled at her and stuck his tongue out. She stuck hers out at him in return.

Sarah was a relieved that her cold war with R.E. was over. But, despite downing coffee each morning, Sarah continued to doze off in her classes as she kept at it. At the end of AP Euro one day in the middle of November, Ms. Smith said to her, "Sarah I would like to talk to you in my office after school."

"Will it take long? I have things to do and need to get home."

"No, it will only take a few minutes."

"Then I'll stop by today."

Later that day she slid into the chair across from Ms. Smith's desk. After playing with her eyeglasses for a moment, Ms. Smith looked directly at her.

"Sarah, I've been deputized by the faculty here, many of whom really like you, to ask you how you are doing. We've noticed that you fall asleep in class, something you've never done before this year. Are you able to handle this thing you've gotten yourself into? You don't have to go through with this, or at least not all the way. You can stop at any time."

"Ms. Smith, thank you for your concern, but I can do this," she said firmly. "As of a couple of days ago, I had fifty-nine applications submitted. I'm on course to finish all one hundred and one on time."

"If you can stay on the course you're on. Sarah, really, you don't have to continue with this," Ms. Smith repeated. "There is nothing dishonorable in stopping. If you submit fifty-nine applications, you will have done more than anyone else."

"I need to do this, Ms. Smith. If I don't get into a good place, I'll look like a complete fool."

"Sarah, your chance of finding a good school is really no different if you complete fifty-nine applications than if you do all one hundred and one. Is there another reason you're doing this?"

"In the process I'll set a record that will probably never be broken. And my relatives and neighbors will be disappointed if I don't apply to the places they've recommended."

"Are you caught up on your class work, including the historiography paper?"

"I'm pretty much up to date in general, and I'm really happy with how my paper has turned out. I'm not going to sacrifice my courses and my grades for this. I'm basically sacrificing everything else."

"That is another point worth talking about. Senior year is the best year most people have in high school. They socialize, go to dances, and usually start dating more heavily. I would hate to see you miss all that."

Sarah was completely taken aback by her last comment because Ms. Smith was notorious for being strictly business.

"It will all be worth it."

"Sarah, it's important, but you can also overemphasize something's importance. Let me tell you a little story. I got a call the other day from a mother who lives in our district. She wanted to know what she needed to do to make sure that her child got into Stanford."

Ms. Smith was a great storyteller, which also made her a great teacher. She paused at just the right moment to let the listener reflect on what she'd said before finishing. Sarah tried to guess who in Oak Stream might be Stanford-fixated.

"This is not the mother of a high school student. This is a mother in the maternity ward of a local hospital who had just given birth. I wanted to go over there and personally strangle her. She will probably completely ruin that child by overthinking the role of college in his life."

It was a sobering story. Sarah thought about it all the way home, and it bothered her for days after that.

What was even more sobering was the discussion near her locker the next week as she was about to leave school for the day. Mike Roberts, a tall blonde guy Sarah knew from middle school, was filling his backpack with what he needed to take home that night. He did not look happy. Another boy, whom she did not recognize, drifted by and started a conversation.

"Hey, Roberts."

"Hey."

"Did you get your Northwestern application in yet?"

"No. Looks like I'm not going to Northwestern."

"What happened? You were really excited about that place."

"That was in September. My dad sat me down last night and talked to me about money. Since October 1st the stock market's dropped about thirty per cent. My parents had a lot of money in stocks, including the money to pay for college, so that's taken a big hit. Basically, they can't pay for me to go there. So I'm thinking about a completely different set of places."

"Man, that sucks. I'm sorry to hear that."

"Yeah, I'm not the only one who got hit by this."

As Sarah walked home in the autumn chill, she thought for a few moments about how it reflected on her situation. Grabbing her cell from her purse, she called R.E.

"Hey, Sarah."

"Hey, what's been going on with the stock market? I haven't been following it."

"It's dropped like a stone. It's like 1929 all over again."

"What about foreign stocks?"

"Even worse than the U.S."

"Are you going to be OK for college?"

He thought for a minute. "My parents aren't really in a position to give me much toward college, so I was going to use money from my savings and take out loans. I'm pretty much unaffected."

"What about Carrie?"

"Sarah, from what I hear, her family has so much money that the market drop, as bad as it is, won't really affect her. They may just take one or two less trips a year, but I don't think it will change Carrie's options. What about you?"

She hesitated before responding. "I don't know. I know we have money in stocks and that Ben's education at Harvard is not cheap. I'll find out tonight. Bye."

Turning up her driveway, Sarah walked to the deck in back of the house.

"Mom, when will Dad be home?" she asked as she came in the backdoor and took off her shoes.

"Same time as usual. Why, is there a problem?"

"I need to talk to him. I've been so busy that I haven't really been paying attention to what's been going on in the economy. It's really bad out there, isn't it?

"It's not pretty, Sarah. But your father's the one with the M.B.A. He can tell you more about it than I can. Do you want me to send him up when he comes in?"

"Yes, please." She shuffled somewhat dejectedly up the steps to her room. For what seemed like hours she played with this and that before finally watching television to kill the time. The afternoon dragged on as she waited for her father to get home.

Around 6:30 p.m. there was a knock on the door.

"Come in," she called as her father entered the room.

"Hi, Sarah. Mom said you wanted to talk to me."

A jumble of words poured out of her mouth: "Dad, I know, or at least I know now, that the stock market has dropped a ton. If you guys don't have the money anymore, I can change my college plans. I can work for a year and then go to school. But I think it's more important that you continue paying for Ben. He's doing great at Harvard, he's in his second year, and it would be really cruel for him to have to stop for a year or work a lot of hours at the same time he's going to college and hurt his grades.

Maybe I can get a job at your office or around Oak Stream somewhere. I know it won't pay much, but it will put money in my pocket, and I promise I'll save most of it for college. I can continue the applications and just defer admission for a year. In the meantime maybe things will turn around. Or if you think it's going to be bad for a while I can consider a whole different set of schools that aren't so expensive. I heard some kids talking in the hall today and I know at least a few of them are doing that. This is really bad, isn't it? We talked about the stock market in AP econ last year and I remember that a thirty percent drop is a big deal. Just tell me what you want me to do, Dad."

"Sarah," he said calmly, "I want you to relax. The long and short of it is that this is why God created bonds."

She gave her father a bewildered look.

"What I'm saying, to put it simply, is that there are two kinds of investments. You can invest in riskless government bonds as opposed to risky investments like common stocks. This is what your mother and I have done with a lot of our retirement funds and other crucial money for years. It's a more conservative strategy and doesn't get you the big gains when the market is up, but it eliminates just this kind of risk. The money that we've promised you for college is there and, in fact, what we have in those mutual funds has increased because the bond market has gone up the last six weeks or so. We'll see what comes after this, but for now it's all OK."

"Oh, Daddy, I was so worried that this was all going to be for nothing." She had not called him "Daddy" for years.

"Sarah, it's all right," he said hugging her gently.

Reassured, Sarah cranked out the applications over the next few days, many nights falling asleep at her desk and having to be awakened by her mother only to move to the bed a few feet away. She had little time to do her hair anymore or pay attention to her appearance or wardrobe. It was work, work, and more work.

Yet she kept at it. By November 26 she had another 14 applications done and felt it was time to meet with Carrie and R.E. the next Saturday. They had not been around much over the past two weeks, but had communicated with Sarah after school mostly by text and e-mail. Carrie, who was a bit of a perfectionist, was putting the finishing touches on her own applications, even though MIT loomed large in her future. R.E., as Carrie and Sarah now called him with some difficulty, was busy with his own plans.

As soon as his name change was final, the former Rob Taylor informed school officials and asked that all his records be changed to reflect this. He asked his letter writers to not mention that he was formerly known as Robert Edward, telling them it would confuse the colleges, and explained that even though he had already applied, it was necessary to reapply as

Running Elk. He apologized profusely for this inconvenience and explained it as bureaucratic nonsense that the universities, in response to his phone calls, insisted was necessary. The teachers, who had never seen a similar case, believed him. The letters were sent, the transcripts quickly followed, and Running Elk immediately submitted his other application materials.

His new name caused varied reactions inside Oak Stream High. As soon as the name change was official, a notice was sent to each of his classes. Most of the teachers thought that a new student had entered the school. Miss Cummings, his English teacher, announced in class one afternoon, "Everyone, we have a new student with us. Mr. Running Elk Taylor. Mr. Taylor, would you care to stand up and say 'hello'?"

"That's me, Miss Cummings."

"But you're Rob Taylor."

"I have legally changed my name, Miss Cummings, to reflect my Native American heritage."

Fate had been cruel to R.E. Taylor by continually putting Tim Tyler in his classes. A senior now, Tim stood 6' 6" and weighed 275 pounds to R.E.'s 160. Tyler, who had earned all state honors in football as a junior and senior and had distinguished himself in the state play-offs this year, had detested Rob since Mr. Harrison's class freshman year.

From his chair in the next row, Tim Tyler turned, raised his right hand and said in a deep tone, "Umm, Running Elk. How."

The other students, even after years of diversity training in grade school and middle school, burst out laughing.

"And how!" R.E. shot back, remembering the standard response from the Three Stooges short film.

The class, appreciating the classics, laughed even louder. This infuriated Tim Tyler to no end because he thought the joke was on him. In the hallway after class, Tyler confronted R.E. at his locker.

"Taylor, you little asshole, what is this Running Elk shit?"

He turned to face the Monster of the Midway.

"That's my legal name."

"Oh, so Rob was like your maiden name?"

"Tyler, why don't you go away? Far, far away."

"Gladly, once I'm done talking to you. By the way, how was the Battle of the Little Big Horn?" he cracked, immediately laughing at his own joke.

"Those were the Sioux, Northern Cheyenne, and some Arapaho. I'm a Potawatomi. Don't you know any history?"

"Potawatomi? Gee, that rhymes with lobotomy," Tyler shot back.

"Oh, that's so funny! Did you think of it by yourself?"

"Screw you."

"Actually, Tim, I'm busy right now. So why don't you go screw yourself?"

Tim Tyler picked him up by the neck with one hand and lifted him high against the closed locker. He looked like he was going to choke the life out of R.E.

At just that moment, Antoine "Twan" Jackson came down the hallway, with Leon Holmes and LaShawn Johnson.

R.E. had tutored Twan in math sophomore year. Twan firmly believed that his B in the class was due to R.E. and was quite grateful.

"Running Elk, my man. What's happening?" Twan asked as his friends moved to either side of him. None of the three were as physically imposing as Tim Tyler, but they were all known around school as tough customers.

Tim Tyler put Taylor down and turned to face them. Despite it being three against one, it would have been one hell of a fight.

"Be cool, Mr. Tyler," Twan Jackson said smoothly to him. Tim Tyler glared at them for 30 seconds before he turned and walked away.

"Antoine, thanks. I think you just saved my life," Running Elk Taylor responded.

"No problem. Us minorities have to stick together," Twan said with a smile. Even the stone-faced LaShawn Johnson laughed. "Haven't seen you around much, Taylor, what have you been up to?"

"I've been mostly working on college applications. Mine and other peoples."

"Oh, yeah, I heard about your friend Sarah. Where are you applying to?"

R.E. rattled off his list of schools.

"Man, those are some impressive places. I wish you luck."

"What about you, Twan?"

"I'm applying to schools named Illinois: Western Illinois, Southern Illinois, Northern Illinois, Eastern Illinois, Illinois State . . ."

"What about the University of Illinois? Have you considered applying there?"

"Do you really think Champaign will take me?

"Why not? Math doesn't come naturally to you, but so what? You're willing to work hard to overcome that. We both know that. Besides, there are lots of things other than math you can major in."

A light went on in Twan Jackson's head. He thought for a moment.

"But what is that gonna cost me?"

"Not much different than the schools you just named. They're all state schools. Twan, you've got your other essays already written. You can probably do the Illinois application in a couple of nights. I've been through it and can help you, if you want. Do you still have my number?"

"Yeah, it's saved in my cell from when you tutored me."

"Call me if you want to do the Champaign application. I'd be happy to help you."

"Let me think about that. I can maybe see myself going there."

Twan gave Running Elk Taylor a fist bump and then headed down the hallway with his friends.

The teachers in R.E.'s other classes gave him peculiar looks but did not comment on his name change, with the exception of his physical education instructor. Norman Nelson, an assistant varsity football coach, was universally despised by the students, including the football players. They called him "Nazi" Nelson behind his back, based on his apparent dislike for much of the human race. The very unathletic Rob Taylor had been lucky in that Nelson–his P. E. instructor since freshman year–had completely ignored him for the preceding three and a half years.

Nelson received the name change form from the principal's office the day he timed the seniors in the 50-yard dash. R.E. Taylor finished dead last among the 25 boys in the class.

"Goddamn it, Taylor, you better pick it up there!" he yelled. "You're never going to make the varsity lacrosse team in the spring with that kind of speed." Then, under his breath, Nelson muttered, "Running Elk, my ass."

That Saturday Sarah got her first three Bauer's gift certificates after reaching the milestone of 75 completed applications. For the first time in what seemed like weeks, Sarah actually relaxed with Carrie and R.E. for a short while around the fire pit in her backyard after they were done that night. Even Thanksgiving had been a workday. Sarah had wolfed down her turkey dinner and pie and had shot back up to her room that Thursday.

She was looking forward to Ben coming home for the holidays, but had no idea when she would see him. Even Kevin was becoming a faint memory, someone she saw only at the dinner table. Just as she was thinking about him, the sliding glass door that separated the deck from the family room opened and Kevin stepped out. He glanced at the three of them on the patio, in their fall jackets, seated around the fire pit. The fire snapped, crackled, and popped as the flames danced around the wood.

"Just wanted to see what you looked like, Sarah," he called out.

"Good-bye, Kevin," she answered back, while poking at the fire with a stick.

"How about some music?" Sarah asked her friends, whose favorite songs were, for convenience, loaded on her Ipod because they spent so much time at her house.

"Sure. How about John Mayer?" Carrie asked.

R.E. grimaced.

"Damn, how about someone who owns a guitar?"

"John Mayer plays the guitar," she retorted.

"Barely," he shot back.

"And your choices are?"

"Jesus and Mary Chain. Blondie. The Replacements. Tom Petty.

Creedence. The Call." R.E. had been raised on classic rock as well as new wave and 80's alternative by his parents.

"Are you aware of any music since John Philip Sousa?" Carrie asked.

"Excuse me. The songs I like are classics for a reason. They've stood the test of time."

"Fine, Sarah. Give him what he wants. I'm way too tired to argue about this."

Sarah compromised by choosing "Dreaming" by Blondie, a song R.E. had introduced them to at homecoming last year, and the three of them, but most of all Sarah, really liked. When it started, Sarah visualized the official video with the arms of the band's drummer, Clem Burke, pounding out the beat at what looked like 100 miles per hour.

"Do you think I'm dreaming, R.E., trying to get in all these top places?" Sarah asked thoughtfully.

"No, I don't think so. Used that way, the word 'dreaming' has a really negative connotation. Sarah, I think you're following your dreams, which is a really positive thing. What would it be like if at our age we didn't have any dreams?"

"If you don't have dreams, all you have are nightmares," Sarah said in response, quoting the character played by Mickey Rourke in the movie *Diner*.

"Exactly."

"Thanks for that. It makes me feel a lot better. What should I play next?"

"JAMC."

Sarah pulled up "Head On" by Jesus and Mary Chain. R.E.'s head bobbed as soon as the song came on. When it finished, she took a deep breath.

"Guys, one more song and then I really have to go to bed because I'm dead tired. What's it going to be?"

"Can you play that mix I made of tunes by the Wacos?"

"Sure."

R.E. had pulled together parts of his favorite songs by the Waco Brothers, who were the kings of punk country music. The MP3 started with "Nothing at All," then rolled into "In Harm's Way" before turning to a delightful little song about going to hell called "Take Me to the Fires." It finished with the complete recording of "Do You Think About Me?" the Waco's version of a song originally done by Lonesome Bob.

As R.E. sang along with his eyes closed, Sarah looked at him bittersweetly. Carrie glanced at Sarah and wondered if she was asking herself the same question.

When the song ended, Carrie and R E. doused the fire and said their good-byes before Sarah dragged herself up to bed.

In late November, Sarah's condition worsened. She began to have a recurring nightmare in which she failed to submit all the applications on time. Even worse, the schools she did meet the deadlines for all rejected her. In desperation she contacted the remaining colleges to ask for an extension. In her dreams, an elderly, gray-haired man with a beard and mustache appeared next and said, "You didn't get all the applications in, did you? Well, that's your problem, not ours. We have rules here–this is academia after all. We're not going to drop everything just for you," he said condescendingly as he tugged on his beard. "So you applied to the top places first to be sure to meet their deadlines. We weren't good enough for you then, were we, but now you want us to worry about you? Maybe the problem is that you're just not cut out for a four-year university. Why don't you try a junior college?"

On the nights the gray-haired man came inside her head, Sarah popped awake long before dawn, shuddering under a perspiration soaked sheet at the prospect of not getting in anywhere, much less at an elite school.

It was also increasingly difficult for her to get out of bed in the mornings and off to class. Because multiple cups of coffee were no longer sufficient to keep her awake, Sarah started taking caffeine tablets before she left the house. She found herself gnawing on pencils and, if she could have seen herself, Sarah would have noticed that she had developed a nervous tic. Her obsession with college applications also took its toll in other areas. She spent less time on her appearance, looking every day a bit more disheveled.

Despite it all, on December 3rd she finished the 80th application. But Sarah crashed physically the next morning. She slept through the alarm, and neither of her parents could wake her. Her mother was in tears in the kitchen, begging Sarah's father to do something.

"John, what the hell is going on with Sarah?" she shrieked. "She's never been this out of it in the morning. We should take her to the doctor. I think she's really physically sick."

John Jennings put down his coffee cup and looked sympathetically at his wife.

"Honey, I know how awful this seems. But she is probably just tired. Haven't you ever slept through your alarm before?"

"Yes, a few times, but only after pulling an all-nighter in college."

"Exactly. You were dead tired but otherwise you were all right." He paused a moment to measure his words before continuing.

"The best thing for Sarah right now is sleep. We'll call her in sick at Oak Stream, let her sleep as long as she wants, and then she can stay home the rest of the day. One day of school won't make any difference."

He kissed his wife on the cheek.

"I have a conference call setup for 9 a.m. at work. Let me phone my office and reschedule it for later in the week."

John Jennings spent the morning drinking coffee and watching television with his wife. Sarah finally awoke around noon and checked the time on the alarm clock.

"Damn it. My alarm didn't go off." She hopped out of bed and ran to the door. "Mom, I've missed half the day at school. Can you drive me?"

Her father walked to the base of the steps.

"Sarah, you slept through the alarm this morning. Your mother and I called you in absent for the day."

Sarah's mind immediately assessed the situation. "OK, I'll call Carrie and have her pick up my homework. I can get notes tomorrow for the classes I missed. I'll just work at home after lunch."

She came down in her pajamas to grab a quick sandwich before going back up to her room. When her mother looked in on her later, Sarah was grinding away again at her college applications.

"She's working on the applications," Mrs. Jennings said in astonishment.

"The sleep helped Sarah. I think I'm going to go into work, unless you really want me to stay here. Can we talk tonight once we have a better idea how she's feeling?"

That evening Kate Jennings, still in a state of anxiety, sat in the study with her husband.

"I'm putting a stop to this, John. This has made a complete wreck of Sarah. You saw how she looked this past week or so in the morning when she went to school—all jittery and fidgety from lack of real sleep and too much caffeine. I'm sorry I ever agreed to let her try this stupid thing."

"Kate, slow down a little. As soon as she got up, Sarah went back to the applications, right? And her progress reports from all her classes are good so she's keeping up with her schoolwork, right? So she still wants to do this and she seems to be managing the work load. She's got eighty applications done and is within striking distance of finishing."

"But look at her; she's a wreck."

"I agree that she looks terrible, but you can't stop her now. Need I remind you that she really wanted to do this, and you wanted to let her try? It would be cruel to make her quit just as she is about to finish. If you make her stop, she's going to really hate you. Let's talk to Carrie and Rob and see what they think before we make a decision."

Some quick phone calls elicited the same opinion from Sarah's closest friends—she seemed to still have things largely under control, and they felt that she should be allowed to see it through.

"Mrs. Jennings, I know this seems bad right now, but if you make her stop, she'll always wonder if she could have finished this," observed Carrie.

However, Carrie kept a closer watch on Sarah, making sure she ate a healthy lunch and reminding her regularly about her homework. When Carrie told Sarah to put on her sweater one day in school, her response was, "You're not my mother."

Sarah received a boost when Ms. Smith handed back the historiography papers. She and R.E. received the two highest grades in the class, with Carrie right behind them. Ms. Smith recommended certain changes to all three and insisted that they submit the revised versions to *Interpretations*. Her AP government paper on constitutional limitations to the war on terrorism was headed there as well, giving Sarah two submissions during the first half of her senior year with a semester still to go.

With renewed energy, Sarah focused on the applications, falling further behind in her class work in the process. She waved Carrie off when asked about it, promising that she would catch up in January. By doing an application a day, on December 10th Sarah had completed 87 apps, and a week later she finished the 94th. All were dutifully checked by Carrie and R.E., who now spent quite a bit of time around her house, having apparently submitted all their own applications. Bakery gift certificates were dispensed on the weekends, with Sarah's father running to Bauer's to fill her requests. A mix of Bauer's, coffee, and caffeine tablets kept her going during the day.

But the gray-haired man invaded her dreams more frequently in December, with the same message each time, sending a chill through her body that always woke her. She confessed to Carrie—on the condition that her mother not be told—that she was having nightmares. But Mrs. Jennings already knew because she heard Sarah call out in her sleep frequently, "Please, just give me one more week! That's all I need! I'll have them done in a week."

Sarah informed her family that they would get gift certificates for Christmas—whenever she had a chance to buy them. Kevin, who enjoyed the extra attention that his sister perennially devoted to his Christmas surprises, sighed loudly when he heard this. At this point Sarah was near exhaustion physically. The only reason that she had not blown up at her parents and Kevin multiple times, such as when dinner was late or the television downstairs was too loud, was because she immediately retreated to her room and put in ear plugs to drown out all external noise. Fortunately, not much was going on in school, and the 19th was the last day of classes in December. It was also the day Ben was coming home. When her parents announced that they would be taking the usual trip to South Bend on December 26th to visit her grandparents, she told them not to count on her. They simply shrugged.

With the finish line in sight, Sarah summoned the energy that remained somewhere deep inside her. Her parents called her in sick on

December 19th, allowing her to tackle the college applications all day. When Ben came home that afternoon, he was appalled by what he saw. Sarah looked like a ghost of herself–thin, pale, and jittery. She muttered a handful of words to him and then excused herself, causing Ben to complain that his sister had become a zombie.

"Ben, we're as concerned about Sarah as you are," his father assured him. "But it's almost over. It's something she decided she really wanted to do, and it looks like she's going to do it. We've always supported you kids in your choices, as you may recall, and in that sense this is no different."

Vermont, Auburn, Northeastern University in Boston, SUNY-Stony Brook, Arizona, University of California-Santa Cruz, and Missouri were the last seven schools on the list. Sarah took them one at a time. The regime of doing one a day helped Sarah immensely at this point because filling out applications had become second nature to her. On Christmas Eve, with the snow falling softly outside her frosted windows as the Christmas lights on her block twinkled in the night, she put the finishing touches on the application to Missouri. Carrie and R.E. had been around her house, either in her room or hanging out with her family a short distance away, for most of the week. It was only fair that they be the first to know that Sarah was done.

"Can you guys come up to my room?" the ghost of Sarah Past asked as she looked into the family room from the steps. She handed them the last seven applications, and, after careful reading, they returned the marked-up copies to her. The changes were made without much trouble, and the forms were submitted electronically.

"You're done!" Carrie shouted, hugging her tightly.

"Sarah, you did it! A few months ago I honestly thought this was completely impossible," R.E. added.

"We have to tell my family," said a rather weak Sarah. Carrie held her arm as they descended the stairs.

"Mom, Dad, Ben, Kevin," Sarah called to them softly. "I just submitted the last application."

"Congratulations, honey," her mother said, putting her arms around Sarah. The individual hug turned into a group hug as her father and brothers crowded around.

R.E. had commissioned a yellow cake with chocolate icing from Bauer's a few days before. He retrieved the white cardboard box from the Jennings's basement refrigerator where it had been stashed away and cut the white string. Written on the top in blue icing was "Sarah" and below that "101!!" Carrie pulled out some candles and a gallon of chocolate milk from a brown grocery bag.

"Look what Rob and Carrie brought." She called him 'Rob' in deference to her parents, who still referred to him by his former name.

The group moved into the kitchen. Kevin, who was as much of a cake fiend as his sister, got out the plates, forks, and a cutting knife as they all took seats around the kitchen table.

"I'm glad you're done with this," Ben said with some remaining apprehension.

"So, does this mean that you're back among the living, Sarah?" Kevin asked.

"Yes, you little goosebrain," she answered with a grin. "I'm going to need some sleep, I think, but this is definitely finished. What time are you planning on opening presents tomorrow?"

"We don't have to do it at the crack of dawn. This year we can all sleep in."

"Thanks, Dad. I may be a little groggy tomorrow though."

"Sarah, we don't care," her father said cheerfully. "We just want to have you back with us."

Sarah cut herself another ample slice of cake.

"Can you wake me in the morning–maybe an hour before you're ready to open presents? And, if you don't mind, after we're done with the cake I'm going to bed. It's eleven o'clock, and I haven't gotten a lot of sleep during the past few weeks."

"Rob, Carrie, since you've been such a tremendous help to Sarah, would you be able to join us tomorrow morning?" Mrs. Jennings asked.

"Gladly," Carrie responded and Rob agreed.

After finishing her cake, Sarah walked her friends to the door.

"I can never thank you two enough. You've both been way beyond great," she gushed while grabbing Carrie around the neck.

"Girl, you did it yourself. We just came along for the ride."

"That's right, Sarah," R.E. agreed, patting her on the back.

"Be quiet, Running Elk," Sarah commanded with a tired smile. She gave him a playful tap on the forehead with her finger in the process. "I owe it all to you two. There is no way I would ever have gotten past thirty applications without you guys."

"Sarah, do you remember our motto?" R.E. asked rhetorically. "The part about 'All for One . . .'?"

"Trust me, I haven't forgotten," Sarah answered. "Guys, I really have to crash right now. I feel worse than awful. So, I'll see you tomorrow?"

They assented before Sarah turned and went up to a much deserved rest.

Her mother shook her awake at 10 a.m. the next day. After a shower and some time doing her hair, Sarah felt better although she was still very tired. At 11 she changed into a different pair of pajamas, in anticipation of falling asleep again after a few hours, and came down to join the assembled group. Carrie and R.E. were sipping hot chocolate in one corner of the family room, removed from the seven-foot Douglas fir covered with ornaments and lights, while her biological family huddled around the tree

"Should we start opening presents?" her father asked on Sarah's arrival.

Mrs. Jennings piled the gifts from the family in front of each person. Ben received a couple of shirts, a watch, and some books. Kevin, who shredded the wrapping paper trying to get at what was inside each box, got video games and clothes. Fluffy received doggie treats and new toys to replace the ones from last year that she had destroyed. The dog huddled near Sarah, craving the attention she had not received in quite some time. Sarah stroked her behind the ears and toyed with her paws. Her parents got the usual things parents give to each other and receive from their children, such as clothing and magazine subscriptions.

Sarah received sweaters and makeup, picked out by her mother, and some history books from her family. Carrie gave her gift certificates to shops in downtown Oak Stream and a handwritten certificate, good for one day of shopping plus lunch and dinner. R.E.'s present was a $25 bakery gift certificate.

"I feel bad that I only have gift certificates for you guys, especially for Carrie and Rob," Sarah complained.

"Actually, we've taken care of them. Ben and I went down to Hyde Park to one of the used bookstores and to Histories and Mysteries over in Forest Home. Augie the owner recommended a bunch of different books to us. For Rob we have *The Normans in European History* by Charles Homer Haskins and Robert L. Nicholson's biography of Tancred and some books on military history by John Keegan. For Carrie we have *The Long Pursuit* by Roy Morris, Jr., which is about Lincoln and Douglas, and some historical fiction written after Dan Brown's *The Da Vinci Code* was published, all of which contain the word Templar in the title. Finally, there is this group of books on Chicago history that you can divide up among yourselves. We really appreciate all the help the two of you gave Sarah and we hope that you like them," John Jennings said.

"These are great," R.E. responded. "Remember, Mr. and Mrs. Jennings, there's evil and there's medieval. Evil is bad. Medieval is good."

Ben shot him that look of pain that young people give to those who use puns, while Sarah's parents laughed at his cleverness.

"Sarah, I am a little concerned about the fact that you'll be here alone while we're at your grandparents. Even though I expect that you'll be sleeping a lot, you'll still need to eat and things."

"Mom, I actually have thought about that. How about if Carrie sleeps over in the guest room? We can hang out when I'm awake–which may not be too often since I made a solemn vow to never drink coffee again."

"I have books to read when you're conked out, Sarah. Plus, I make a mean can of Campbell's chicken soup. Mrs. Jennings, I'll make sure she eats right and cleans her room, and I'll do the laundry and dishes. We can also use our faithful Indian companion, oops, I mean our Native American companion, Running Elk, as an errand boy when we need to."

Ben shook his head, still not sure what the name change was about.

"That's right, Mrs. Jennings. I'll be around during the holidays and can be over here during the day. I can open a can of soup just as well as Carrie can."

"All right, but no wild parties," Mrs. Jennings playfully admonished them.

"Nothing wilder than reading history books," Carrie responded.

It wasn't much longer before Sarah started to nod off. She went back up to bed and slept until the next morning, rising to tell her family good-bye. Carrie came over shortly after that with her stuff and settled in. R.E. dropped by later, but sensing from Carrie's behavior that she wanted to speak to Sarah alone, he drifted into another room and read.

"I actually like the idea of staying over here and taking care of you, Sarah. My mother is driving me completely crazy," Carrie stated while pulling at her hair. "I never really had a chance to say too much during the last few months because you were so focused on what you were doing, but she's done nothing but complain about the fact that I applied to places other than MIT. She doesn't get it. I mean, who applies to just one place?"

"Not me," Sarah said with a big smile. She sat in an oversized chair with her legs crossed. "Will it get better next year when you're away at school?"

Carrie was greatly relieved to see Sarah smiling again.

"I have no idea. It's never been any other way. I feel like my life is so planned out. I can picture the moment I was born. Instead of the nurses wrapping me in a blanket when I came out of the womb, I'm sure my mother jumped up from the hospital bed, wrestled me from their arms, and dressed me in a little MIT logo outfit."

"Can you talk to your mother?"

Carrie gave her a stupid look.

"What about your dad?"

"He's never home."

"Is he in the Mideast again this week?"

"No, that was last week and the three weeks before that. This week it's Brussels. Then apparently he is in Asia next week. Even when he is around, he pretty much delegates all this to my mother."

"That is really kind of awful."

"Yes, it is. I wish I had your parents, Sarah. They are so OK with what you choose."

"Mostly, although I think they were getting pretty worried about me, especially because Ben was on their case about the application thing. But at least this part, which is usually the hard part of the process, is over now—for both of us."

"Well, not exactly. I haven't submitted my application to MIT yet."

"Carrie, what are you waiting for? There are only a couple of days left!"

"I don't know. I'm really uncomfortable with this all being determined for me in advance, without me having any say in it. If I don't apply to MIT, they can't let me in, right?"

Sarah gasped. "How are you going to pull that off? With your mother constantly hanging over you, isn't she going to know that you didn't submit it? I'm surprised that she's let it go this long—or that she hasn't written it and submitted it for you."

Sarah had never liked Carrie's mother because she felt that Mrs. Wilson treated her daughter extremely unfairly.

"All right I guess I'll submit it. After I fix dinner I can go back home and do it."

Carrie seemed distracted while she made spaghetti and salad in the kitchen. The girls ate in silence. R.E. was off helping his father on a project at home.

Suddenly Carrie's facial expression changed.

"I just got an idea. But it's probably going to take me a few hours to work it out. I have to run home. Don't touch the dishes; I'll do them later," Carrie shouted over her shoulder as she bolted out the backdoor after dinner.

It was several hours before she returned holding a manila folder in her hand.

"Sorry it took me so long, Sarah, but I've been thinking some more. Like you said, I have to apply to MIT. But they don't have to accept me. Voila, I give you my new admissions essay to MIT—what I refer to as 'The Essay from Hell'."

She opened the folder and handed two pieces of paper to Sarah who was sitting on the couch. They read:

Describe the world you come from, for example your family, clubs, school, community, city, or town. How has that world shaped your dreams and aspirations?

I can describe the world I come from in two words: "It sucks."

My father is a successful—according to the capitalist definition of the word—engineer who works for a multinational construction entity. He helps them build major facilities, grossly exploiting the working man in the process, which are used by the military-industrial complex almost surely to manufacture land mines, which maim small children and smaller animals around the planet, and napalm, which makes it easier for our fascist military to kill the innocent indiscriminately. He's not home very much, probably because he needs to bribe the whores of the capitalist system, our "elected" representatives in Washington, on a regular basis. That's when he's not in Iraq helping the previously mentioned harlots waste billions of dollars in the pursuit of cheaper (and ozone-eroding) oil to power the oversized vehicles that American males insist on driving to try and compensate for deficiencies in certain parts of their anatomy. .

My mother is a classic capitalist Stepford wife. Her life consists of advancing my father's career and generating more filthy lucre for the Wilson family. She hosts endless parties for the people he works with as well as his clients, obsequiously groveling before them in the hope that it will get us another dime. I abhor her shameless ass-kissing of the people my father reports to, who are the dispensers of money in the corrupt American gulag.

My community? I live in Oak Stream, which is so hip that it now actually lets minorities live here. Well, aren't we "with it"? Unless, of course, this is just done for the convenience of the capitalist puppet masters who control the system. Maybe we need a few token blacks and Latinos around to shine our shoes, do our laundry, operate a restaurant specializing in ribs or tacos when we need to eat ethnic food, or to play some blues or salsa music when we feel like showing how inclusive we are.

How has this shaped me? It totally repulses me, and I live my life with one aspiration; to wipe away the filth my parents live in.

I'm repulsed by the capitalist system and everything associated with it. Like a drunk who has vomited up the last drop in his stomach, I'm sickened beyond being sick. I work daily for the overthrow of the economic status quo and its replacement with a pure communist state described in the works of Marx and Lenin, an event which is coming soon, as the crippled system known as capitalism cannibalizes itself through erosion of capital in the stock and housing markets.

I'm repulsed by my parents and their materialistic needs. I completely reject their wealth, which was stolen from the workers through their positions as loyal capitalist lackeys. When they finally die, which unbeknownst to them will set them free from their puppet masters and make them better people, I plan to donate all their assets to start a workers' commune in Cuba or Albania. It may be too late to save my parents in the next world they so firmly believe in, but it will cleanse at least my soul of their endless sins.

I'm repulsed by everything about my parents. I reject the subservient role this society has forced on my mother in favor of radical feminism rooted in a Marxist-Leninist (with a sprinkling of Maoist) ideology. I reject their blind adherence to the monogamous, heterosexual credo put forth by Anglo-Saxon religion, one of the main tools of the Western capitalist states, which they practice in the Oak Steam gulag. As soon as I'm beyond my parents' sight, I intend to throw off the archaic sexual shackles imposed on them and engage in rampant bisexualism with an infinite number of partners, if my other commitments allow me time to do so. In short, I reject their lives completely.

The only dimension on which I disagree with Marx is that religion is the opiate of

*the masses. In the U.P.S.A.—the United Puppet States of America—currently college
education is the drug used to control the masses. The bulk of our youth go on to state-
controlled—either directly or indirectly—institutions for four years to be indoctrinated in the
idea that capitalism is the only economic system and that it can not be questioned. They
become mindless automatons, capable of living their lives only as stockbrokers, bankers,
accountants, and engineers. In other words, they are brainless pawns of the system.*

*If I'm admitted to MIT, my first act, during orientation week, will be to take over
the administration building. I will demand that every course at the school, from
accounting to zoology, not only cover material in the discipline but also discuss the context
that the discipline exists in—the corrupt American corporate state. If my demands are not
met, I will blow the building up. If somehow I am stopped, I will wreak vengeance on the
campus as soon as I'm able to return, no matter how long it takes.*

Those are my dreams and aspirations.

"What do you think of it?" Carrie asked.

"Jesus. It reads like something the Unabomber might have written, if
he was a woman and PMS-ing."

"Excellent. Do you think it will get me rejected by MIT?"

"Carrie, if Bush or Cheney see it, it will probably get you imprisoned in
Guantanamo Bay immediately," Sarah replied.

"Outstanding!" she exclaimed.

"Unfortunately, though, it won't solve your problem."

"Why not?"

"Your mother knows every dean in the admissions office there, right?"

"At Guantanamo Bay? I don't think so."

"No, silly, at MIT. She sends them cards on their birthdays and
presents at Christmas. She knows their spouses and the names and birth
dates of all their children. She has been contributing big money to the place
since you were little to ensure your spot there. What do you think is going
to happen if they reject you?"

"She'll call them up and complain."

"Complain, Carrie? She'll make more noise than the goddamn
Hiroshima blast!"

"But they seriously won't admit me, will they?"

"I bet they will."

"Those unbelievable bastards, how could they do that?"

"Think about it from their perspective; it's the smart move. If they
admit you, your mother can't complain. She got what she paid for."

"But I'm threatening to blow up the campus, for Christ's sake."

"I think they will shrug that off. The children of the wealthy, and your
family is fairly well-to-do, are always revolting against something or other.
Remember Patty Hearst? Or how about Jane Fonda? After all those years
criticizing the 'system,' she ends up marrying Mr. I Am the System, Ted

Turner." Sarah stopped for a moment to think. "Put yourself in their shoes. Let's say they take your essay somewhat seriously as a statement of your current beliefs. If they accept you, as far as they know you might not come. So they are safe there. If you do come, you may be a little trouble when you're an undergraduate, but you'll probably do a Jane Fonda later—and bequests to universities are generally made later in life. So they get a good chunk of Wilson money some years after you graduate. I bet you they accept you."

Carrie frowned as what Sarah said sank in.

"I think you have to play this one straight, Carrie. No matter how easy it might seem, not submitting the app or sending them that essay will not solve your problems, given what your mother is like."

"I guess you're right. Besides, MIT is number four on that list you used. So how bad can it really be there?"

"Good point, Carrie. Come on, cheer up. Hit the submit button tomorrow on the MIT app and we'll both be done with this part of the process. We'll have lots more free time."

"We should try and have some fun next semester," Carrie suggested. "After all, we're seniors."

"You're right. Once I catch up on my sleep and my course work, fun is the order of the day. What should we do?" Sarah asked, fluffing a pillow behind her. "I know. We can date boys."

"In your dreams, Sarah," Carrie said with a look of total disbelief. "How many guys have been interested in us so far? We're too smart. They're afraid of us. And in my case any guys who have ever gone out with me, even in the eighth-grade style of just doing things as part of a larger group of kids, got the Spanish Inquisition from my mother, which caused them to flee immediately."

"Nobody expects the Spanish Inquisition," Sarah said sternly, quoting the tag line from a hilarious sketch by *Monty Python's Flying Circus*.

"Ah, and need I remind you how much guys appreciate not just smart girls but also sarcastic ones? Plus we don't dress slutty or fawn all over them to attract their attention. Sarah, my dear, I'm afraid we're destined to be old maids. Or, my dear, in your very Catholic case, a nun."

"OK, Carrie, we can have fun in other ways. We'll go downtown to Macy's or out to Oakbrook shopping. We can take the El to museums. R.E. will come along too."

Sarah slept 10 to 12 hours each of the next few nights and often dozed off in front of the television during the day. She was happy to watch TV and read, refusing Carrie's offer to go on a shopping expedition. By December 30th Sarah felt partly restored. She looked better, and her recently acquired bad habits were gone. Fun consisted of making popcorn, ordering pizza, and watching (or at least having on the television) the endless stream of college bowl games. Sarah looked forward to her parents coming back on the 31st. A blanket of snow had fallen on Chicago a few days before, and she had taken Fluffy for long walks, which she had not done for quite some time, in this winter wonderland. R.E. accompanied her.

"So, when will we hear from these places?" she asked R.E., meaning the colleges.

"It's pretty much going to happen at the end of March, except for the schools with rolling admissions or some other form of making earlier decisions. For me, that means I'll hear from Michigan and Illinois probably in January some time. For you, you'll start to get answers in January, but the bulk of the responses will come around April first."

"April Fool's Day. How appropriate."

9
CAMPUS VISITS AND ... WAITING

New Year's Eve, when Sarah's family returned, and the following day, were quiet ones in the Jennings house, with the exception that her father suggested that they that take another short trip that weekend, saying, "Sarah, you've missed not only the holidays with the family, but you've also been 'gone' the entire fall. How about if we get up early this Saturday and, if the weather cooperates, run up to South Haven? We can spend the night there and drive back by noon on Sunday, giving you plenty of time to get ready for school on Monday."

For many of the past 15 years, her family had vacationed during the summer in South Haven, Michigan, on Lake Michigan's eastern shore. They usually rented a small house on the south side close to downtown, away from the party atmosphere on the north side, and hung out on South Beach. Some of her earliest memories were of the red lighthouse at the end of the pier and playing in the sand with Ben.

"That would be great," she gushed. "But it's the dead of winter."

"All the better," her brother Ben interjected as he entered the kitchen where the family was gathered. "We can get into Clementine's and get Sherman's ice cream in town without having to worry about the lines. It will give you some time to reconnect with us."

"Don't you have to go back for Reading Week or whatever it's called?"

"Final exams don't start until January thirteenth. I fly back on the sixth of January and I have my class notes with me here, so I'll be fine."

Everyone agreed that South Haven would be fun. When they arrived on Saturday, after a quick lunch, Ben asked Sarah if she would take a walk on South Beach with him. Since the wind was calm and the sun was bright, she gave in.

"Sarah," Ben said as they passed the brick pumping station, along the driveway down to the beachfront parking, and stepped on to the whitish sand, "you really can not decide on a university or attend one without ever having set foot on one."

"Ben, I've planned this out and I'm sticking to my plan. The applications are in, and we'll see which universities admit me. I have quite a bit of time before I need to make a decision and I don't want to talk about this stuff right now, thank you very much," she said, giving him a cross look. She was getting a bit tired of her "knowledgeable" older brother telling her what to do.

"Sarah, cards on the table. Part of the reason we came down here on short notice this weekend was to get you out of the house and as far away from the process as possible so you can think clearly. Mom and Dad agree with me on this. You should make some visits."

"I have to get back to my schoolwork since I'm taking AP Euro, along with AP this and that, and finals are coming up."

They continued down the beach, where they had often searched for unusual colored rocks and sea glass, as they called broken pieces of bottles and other glass fragments worn smooth by the waves and sand.

"What about after that? You'll have some time."

"Fine," she said, grabbing her head to avoid screaming. "If it makes you and Mom and Dad happy—all of whom are not directly involved in this decision—I will visit some campuses. Now will you please shut up about it?" She immediately turned around and walked back down the beach toward the house they were renting.

The rest of their stay there and the ride home were as frosty as the temperature, the only bright spot being a trip downtown when Sarah took Kevin to get ice cream.

When they returned home on Sunday, she arranged to go over to Carrie's. In the past when Sarah had had parental issues, she'd always found the much suffering Carrie to be the best person to confide in. They hid out in Carrie's room, her inner sanctum in her own parental maelstrom, and talked.

"God, I thought I was going to get some relief here—for a few months anyway—and revert to being Sarah Jennings, high school kid. But I let my guard down for one minute, and there's college sneaking up on me."

"Sarah, relax. Seriously, the problem is easily solved. You can visit Chicago and Northwestern. The demands by all parties are then completely satisfied."

"I'm certainly not going with either of my parents after they forced this on me. But I don't think I can get motivated enough to drive by myself."

"Don't worry about it. I'll go with you, even though I already visited

Chicago last year," Carrie volunteered. "I've got my MIT trip right after finals are over, during the weekend starting January 23rd. After that we'll hit Chicago one day and Northwestern another. If you want, but you don't have to, you can cash in your gift certificate from me for Christmas for one day in Hyde Park. I assume they have edible food there, somewhere. Plus, as a special offer, I'll throw in an identical one for Northwestern. We'll make a day of it in both cases."

"Carrie, would you? I mean would you do that just for me?" Sarah gushed.

"Yes, I would. I know what insistent parents are like and how stressed you are. Besides, 'All for One,' right?"

"Thank you," Sarah responded softly, giving Carrie a hug.

Scanning the school calendar, they chose February 13th and February 16th, both of which were official non-attendance days at Oak Stream, for Sarah's only two campus visits.

They returned to school on January 5, 2009, with roughly two weeks until the three-day final exam period began on January 20. Feeling somewhat behind, Sarah studied like she had never studied before, going over her class notes multiple times and re-reading and outlining textbook chapters. But even that was more relaxing than doing college applications. By the 20th, after some long sessions with R.E. and Carrie, she felt ready.

She also made sure to bring some nice gift certificates to Ms. Smith, Mr. Harrison, and Mr. Williams, to thank them for writing letters for her, and sent a basket of fruit to the office in school that handled the transcript requests.

Carrie flew to Boston on the red eye on the morning of the 23rd as soon as finals were over. Her Friday afternoon consisted of the usual college visit items, such as a guided tour of the campus and the opportunity to sit in on some classes. She arranged to stay over for the weekend with Lauren Bates, her classmate Kathy Bates's very studious older sister, who was a sophomore at MIT.

The tour was like every campus tour she had been on before. It meandered about the quads, with the guide pointing out buildings and items of interest, and even swung by the imposing structure donated by one of her forefathers. The starkness of it made her shudder a bit. At the end they were back in the admissions office in a meeting room for a question-and-answer session. Their guide, a preppie-looking young woman with brown hair and light skin, was good at fielding questions and putting the proper spin on her answers. Most of the questions were fairly mundane, and Carrie learned little from them.

"I've heard that it's very competitive here," stated a prospective male student who sat a few feet in front of Carrie and took detailed notes the entire time. "Is that true?"

"When you have some of the finest young minds in the country together at the same place, in a competitive environment, such as classes in which a fixed percentage of the students get an A, yes, there is strong competition. Everyone is trying very hard to excel, and students are evaluated relative to one another. But don't you want to be at a place where you can compete with the best?"

"Let me rephrase my question," the young man continued, holding his jaw while he searched for the right words. "I've heard that it's not just competitive, as you describe it, but that it's very cutthroat."

"I'm sure that many things people have heard about MIT are completely exaggerated. Just like not everyone at a state school is a hard-partying fraternity member, and not everyone who goes to school in California is a surfer who spends all his time at the beach."

When the session broke up, Carrie headed over to the student union in search of a diet Coke. She was supposed to meet up with Lauren Bates around dinnertime. After paying at the cash registers, she sat at the empty half of a big table in the fairly crowded hall. Six younger looking students, who from their appearance and demeanor were only a year or two older than Carrie, were seated at the other end, chatting away.

"I've got a good story for you guys," said an animated boy to his friends. He had thick-framed glasses and looked like he belonged in the sciences. "There's this freshman on my floor, Robert, who took a chemistry class last fall that the guy down the hall from me, Eugene, took the previous year. The teacher was rumored to use almost the same midterm over and over. So Robert, whom Eugene does not like, asks Eugene for a copy of his old midterm. Eugene stalls him so that he can create what looks like the midterm, but it actually has completely different questions on it from other areas than what the real midterm asked about. He gives the fake midterm to Robert, who memorizes the answers thinking he has it nailed. When Robert goes to the class, the professor passes out the same exam that Eugene actually took. Robert locks up when he sees the exam is different and bombs it. It messes up his course grade and puts him on academic probation. Welcome to MIT, Robert."

"Wow," one of the girls in the group intoned.

"I have a good one," a slender Asian girl with a pretty face offered. "Last year, in the dorm room next to me, there were these two girls who were really not getting along. They barely spoke to each other and obviously they were planning on not rooming together this year. But the one girl had to write an end-of-term paper for her history class that counted a lot toward the course grade. Her roommate let her get it almost finished. Then when she was gone, her roommate deleted it from her computer and from her backup. The first girl knew what had to have happened to it and threw a fit. They had an absolute brawl in the hallway, with kicking, punching, and hair pulling. The "b" word, the "c" word, the "f" word, and the "s" word were all flying. Finally the resident head separated them, and the campus police came. The first girl complained to the cops and the administration, but since she didn't see her roommate do it she couldn't prove anything against her."

"Wow!" the same girl as before exclaimed.

"I think I have a better one," said a mousy blonde girl. "Now, I can't vouch for this being true because I don't know either of the two girls involved, but I heard it from everybody in my dorm last year, and they knew the main actor in this. There was this senior physics major last year, who was sleeping with the T.A. in her Quantum Mechanics III class."

"So what?" one of the guys at the table interrupted the story. "That's hardly novel around here."

"Let me finish," the blonde shot back. "The girl involved with the T.A. and another girl in the class were both top students who were under consideration for a really prestigious summer research position after the class was over. The second girl, the one who wasn't sleeping with the T.A., at least not to anyone's knowledge, was apparently a bit ahead in terms of grade point average before this class started. But the first girl did such a good job on the T.A., she not only convinced him to give her an A, but she got him to grade everything the other girl turned in down so that she got a B. Girl Number One ended up getting the position by sabotaging her competitor."

"Wow, that is a good story," said one of the listeners. All the MIT students at the table agreed.

"Excuse me. Are those really true stories, or are you guys joking?" Carrie asked, turning toward the group.

"You don't go here?" the mousy blonde asked. She seemed surprised by the question.

"I'm just visiting a friend from high school for the weekend. She's a sophomore here." Carrie lied convincingly, not wanting to let on that she was a prospective student for fear that they might clam up.

"Yeah, those are all true, to the best of our knowledge."

"So you would say that MIT is a very cutthroat place?"

"Definitely. Some kids here are really out to get ahead."

"Absolutely," a boy from China added. "You have to be careful who you decide to trust here as well as just watching your back in general."

"I was not aware of that," Carrie answered in all seriousness.

At dinner she asked Lauren about the campus atmosphere, just in case what she'd heard at the student union, although true, might not be representative of MIT overall.

"Carrie, those are not isolated stories. You hear things like that a lot on this campus, and I don't think it is as common elsewhere, based on talking to the Oak Stream kids I know at other universities."

"God, that is so mean," Carrie concluded.

"Welcome to MIT, Carrie," Lauren replied.

It was a long, sobering plane ride home as Carrie pondered this information. When Sarah picked her up at O'Hare, Carrie repeated what she'd heard to her.

"Wow," Sarah exclaimed.

"Yes," Carrie said, "that seems to be the standard reaction to the pirates' den known as MIT. I don't think I want to go to a place that is so damn cutthroat."

"How will your mother feel about that?"

"That presents certain problems. You know how obsessed she is about me being a student there," Carrie said, wrinkling her brow. "Let's see where else I get in before I worry about it anymore."

During the last week of January, the Oak Stream *Sentinel* ran a short piece entitled "Sarah Jennings Gets It Done" on the second page. It read:

As promised, the Sentinel is keeping tabs on Sarah Jennings. To the surprise of many, she completed all 101 applications on time, submitting the last one on Christmas Eve. Now, like the rest of us, she is waiting to hear who will admit her. Then she needs to make the big decision about where to go. But according to Sarah, who was contacted by this writer by telephone, "College will be easy after this." We will keep you posted.

That same week, a very new, boyish looking admissions officer at the University of Illinois walked into his boss's office with a stack of folders containing applications. The room, which could have used a fresh coat of paint, was about as pleasant as the person in it.

"Sit down, Charlie," the assistant dean commanded. Kate Halligan was around 50 years of age, with a stern demeanor and non-smiling Irish eyes that reminded her underlings of a tough old nun.

Charlie Wells caught himself just in time and refrained from responding, "Yes, Mother Superior." She would not have appreciated him calling her that or Mother Condescending, her other nickname in the admissions office.

"Kate, I've finished this batch of applications. Would you like to review them?"

Carrie, Sarah, and Rob's manila folders were in the pile.

"No, I would not," was the reply. "You really don't have to lug the folders around with you all over creation. You can leave them in the file cabinets where they belong. Otherwise they'll get lost. I'll review the spreadsheet summarizing the applications, assuming that you've prepared one, and, if I need to see a file, someone can pull it for me. Now, tell me briefly about these."

"All of them, fifty in total, are admits. Should I prepare acceptance letters notifying them that they're in?"

"No, you should not. Have you checked the names against the Clout List?"

"What list?"

"The Clout List. Surely you've heard from your peers about the list we have?"

The expression on his face said "No." She gave him a pained look.

"You see, Charlie, this is the University of Illinois. We are a state-supported institution, meaning that every year part of what we spend is allocated to us by the legislature through the state budget. Therefore, various influential people contact us regarding students they want admitted to the university."

Charlie Wells was a bit surprised because his expectation had been that academia was a rather pristine environment.

"Out of curiosity, just who are these people?"

"Oh, the governor, the legislators, politicians around the state, people on the board of trustees, lobbyists connected to the governor, big time donors in both political parties . . . basically every pimp and whore in the state."

"Has this been going on for a long time?"

"Not at this extreme level. It really ramped up under our esteemed governor, the 'Honorable' Rod Blagojevich." She made "Honorable" sound like the dirtiest word in the English language. "You see, the board of trustees, which oversees the university system, used to be elected by the people of the state. They were a pretty independent group and weren't afraid to stand up to political pressure. A few years ago they switched it so that the trustees are appointed by the governor. This is a very servile bunch."

"And we let people in just because they're on this list?"

"You bet we do. Since you're new here, let me explain something to you; Illinois is the most corrupt state in the union."

"I thought Louisiana was."

"Oh, that's a false impression fostered by the fact that Louisiana politicians have historically done a much better job of getting caught and convicted than our pols have. But don't despair. Rod Blagojevich, with help from the U.S. Attorney's office, is going to fix all that."

"Does this go on anywhere else?"

Kate Halligan glanced at her watch to make sure that she did not need to be somewhere else.

"To some extent, yes. Every university admits people for reasons that have nothing to do with their academic qualifications. For example, if you're a legacy at a private school, you have a better chance of getting admitted than a similar applicant without family ties to the university."

She twisted her face strangely as an ancient memory drifted into her mind.

"When I started out in this field, I was working at a private university west of here. The dean of the school of business admitted someone to the M.B.A. program in response to a phone call from the chancellor. His parents were big donors to the university."

"From what you just said, that doesn't sound too unusual."

"Oh yes, it was. When you take into account that this young man did not have a bachelor's degree, it was quite unusual."

"I thought you had to have a bachelor's degree to get a master's degree."

"Not if your family donated a lot of money to the university."

"So this kid never finished his bachelor's degree?"

"Actually, he never started it. He had never been to college."

"Oh my God. And they let him in?"

"You bet they did. The dean of the business school was a fairly spineless person who jumped every time the chancellor called him."

"But isn't the use of clout kind of unfair?"

"It is to the people who get displaced by those with clout. They have to go somewhere else. That may not matter so much at a private school. If you don't get into X because some kid with clout gets your spot, you go to Y. And there are lots of Ys of similar quality that cost about the same. But if a kid who lives in Illinois does not get in here, he will likely go to a private school or a public school out of state to get the same quality education. So he ends up paying private school tuition or out-of- state tuition at some other public university, both of which are a lot higher than Illinois in-state tuition."

"That's a lot of money."

"Yes, it is."

"OK, I'll look at the list in the future before I deny an application."

"No, you don't understand. You need to check it even for the admits. If they're on the list, we may have to give them a scholarship."

"Good Lord, that's sick."

"Yes, it is. Let's hope the papers never get wind of this. They'll crucify us."

When the Chicago newspapers did find out about the Clout List, crucifixion was a fairly mild term for what happened to the University of Illinois higher ups.

In early February Sarah received letters from Illinois and Michigan. She was accepted by both schools, as were Carrie and Running Elk Taylor. Robert Edward Taylor got a split decision; Illinois admitted him, but he was rejected by the University of Michigan at Ann Arbor.

"All right," Sarah said with a gigantic smile. "We've all been admitted to at least one good school. No matter what happens after this, we're in good shape."

R.E. smiled in return, but Carrie only frowned.

The celebrity status that Sarah had achieved based on the Associated Press article did not seem to factor into the decisions at Illinois and Michigan, who treated her like any other candidate. But unbeknownst to her, other schools took notice. It started at Harvard and spread from there.

One Monday morning the admissions committee at Harvard met to discuss a batch of applications. An associate dean cleared his throat near the end of the meeting and remarked, "I should mention that in this group, which comes as no great surprise given her application strategy, we also have Sarah Jennings who lives near Chicago—the so-called 'Girl Who Applied Everywhere.' It's basically a fairly ordinary application. She's in the top five percent or so in her class, albeit strong in history, about a 95th percentile on her board exams, and some decent but unremarkable extracurricular activities. I presume that we will not be admitting her. The only thing unusual about her is this gimmick of applying to over one hundred universities, which strikes me as an attempt to set some sort of record."

The dean of undergraduate students, at the head of large wooden table in a beautifully paneled conference room with stained glass windows, sat up slightly straighter than before. He looked directly at the associate dean.

"Actually, I think that we will be admitting her. She is a celebrity, after all, and Lord knows Harvard has admitted quite a few of those, from the grandson of the Aga Khan to numerous members of the Kennedy family. We should be grateful at least that she's not Paris Hilton. Plus, what she did, although a bit madcap, does show a certain type of determination. If she can get that done, she can probably finish any task undergraduate life throws in front of her."

"Do you think she can handle the work load here?" the associate dean asked.

"Oh, I think so. Most of the people who apply here can handle the course work. It's just a question of which ones we decide to let in. As you know, for every one applicant we let in there are easily another five we reject who are probably just as good. After all, how much information do we really have about these kids? Every place is different so it's hard to interpret their high school records. And not every high school offers a full range of AP classes, so we can't compare them on that. The one true standardized measure we have is the SAT, because they all take it. But that's a very imperfect predictor of undergraduate performance," the dean said with great candor. "She's bright enough and will be studying the field she has a passion for. Plus, she has a brother here who is doing quite well. He should be able to help her out if necessary, especially because he will be here during her first two years before she focuses just on history. When her letter is ready to go out, see if you can get the brother to persuade her to come here."

The associate dean moved Sarah's folder of application materials from one pile to another.

A week later an assistant dean at Stanford heard that Harvard was going to admit Sarah. He reported it to his boss.

"Do you know this for a fact?" the boss asked.

"No, it's just a rumor at this point."

"What's your source?"

"A woman who works at MIT who has contacts at Harvard," the assistant dean responded.

"We need to find out for sure. It's not good to fall behind in the celebrity arms race." The Stanford higher-up thought for a moment. "We just received a resume from an admissions officer at Harvard who's looking for a job here because his wife is joining the chemistry department." He pulled a copy off his desk and passed it to his underling. "Call him up. At home, not at work. You should be able to squeeze him for information because he wants a job. Find out if they are admitting her and, secondly, if they are offering her any money. Then check over at Berkeley on the same two things. We want to be in the same ballpark as Harvard and we really don't want her going to Berkeley if we can help it."

The assistant dean reported back to his boss in a few days.

"The guy you asked me to call was quite helpful after I promised him I would mention it to you personally. Harvard is admitting her, but they are not offering her any grants or scholarships—just a weekend out there on them so that her brother can try to convince her to enroll. Apparently they think that will close the deal."

"Then I think we better admit her," the Stanford dean concluded. "What about our 'friends' in the smoke-filled environment on the east side of the bay?"

"Berkeley is going to admit her. But they're not offering her any money."

"Then admit her, but no money. We should dominate Berkeley, unless she's some sort of pot head, and we're competitive with Harvard."

"If I may make a suggestion? What if we give her around $10,000 a year? We would easily dominate Harvard and totally dominate Berkeley."

The dean sat back in his chair and touched the tips of his fingers on both hands together, which made him appear to be praying. He spoke to his staff member with the air of the master instructing the pupil.

"But we don't want her that bad. There are any number of Caucasian applicants who, if we give them that money, will surely come here and be eternally—and more importantly, monetarily—grateful later in life. She's a history major, so she's unlikely to be another Hewlett or Packard. And she will probably come here if we give her what Harvard offers because we're the more desirable place. You see, it's a question of doing the most with the resources we have."

Nonetheless, the assistant dean from Stanford bragged to his colleagues, after a few too many Heinekens at a San Francisco bar that Friday night, that Stanford was admitting one of the year's celebrity applicants and that she was likely to enroll. One of the people at the table was, unbeknownst to the rest, applying for a job in the admissions office at Berkeley. The information filtered across the bay immediately and hit the gossip superhighway, also known as e-mail, shortly thereafter.

As word spread through the university admissions community that Harvard and Stanford, with Berkeley in tow, were going to admit Sarah Jennings, a number of other places grabbed her folder, sometimes out of the deny or wait list pile, and re-examined it.

At Washington University in St. Louis, a stuffy, overfed associate dean asked a staff member to track down Sarah's file when he heard the news. She scurried out of his office and came back in about half an hour.

"I found it. It's already been looked at, and the provisional decision is to admit," the young woman said, summarizing the case.

"Yes, Karen," the associate dean intoned while tugging on his beard. "But now she's going to be admitted by Harvard and Stanford, plus Berkeley, which means many other top schools will admit her. Which means she will probably choose one of them rather than us. This won't do at all. If we admit her and she goes elsewhere, that will hurt our percentage of admits who matriculate. Which will make us look like a less desirable place in the eyes of future applicants and admits. Which means less of them will come here, leading to less alumni, less alumni donations, and a smaller endowment. We really need to worry about the endowment, given how the market has dropped and that the investment advisor for some of our biggest donors "made off" with a lot of their money. We can't live on what our founders made in the fur trade forever, you know. So we absolutely have to reject her."

The staffer, Karen, had always wondered why a grown man wore a coonskin cap to work. She scurried back down the hall to inform the relevant admissions officer that what was once good was now decidedly bad.

By February 13, with their fall semester final exams behind them and the results as expected, the girls were ready to make Sarah's campus visits. Carrie, who knew the South Side a bit, drove her car east toward the downtown and then south on the Dan Ryan Expressway. Passing the stadium where the White Sox played, which a segment of the people living in Oak Stream regarded as a holy shrine, they exited on 55th street and soon snaked through Washington Park which bordered the Hyde Park neighborhood on the west. A wonderful sculpture by Lorado Taft called *The Fountain of Time* came into view just before they turned onto the Midway Plaisance, which had been a central area of the 1893 World's Fair. Carrie found a parking place at the far end, near the giant statue dedicated to Tomas Masaryk, the Czech president whose son died under mysterious circumstances. The brooding, gray winter sky hanging over Hyde Park matched the gray buildings on Chicago's campus.

They started with a brief information session held in one of the imposing Gothic structures just north of the Midway. As they entered the room, Carrie and Sarah spotted Frank Foster sitting in the back. He smiled at them, and they waved as they found a couple of empty seats near the front, between the high school kids who were there with a parent. The presentation, as Carrie whispered to Sarah, was fairly standard, describing the school and its programs, except for the mention of the inordinate number of Nobel Prizes won by Chicago faculty and others associated with the university. The 30-year-oldish male admissions officer, after firmly emphasizing Chicago's rich Nobel harvest, opened it up for questions.

The first one came from a well-dressed parent sitting with two boys and another parent in the row behind Carrie and Sarah. "In your admissions process, how do you take account of the fact that a student might be from a prestigious high school, such as New Baden, as opposed to a high school in Podunk, Ohio?"

New Baden was a posh suburb north of the city with an excellent public high school by the same name. Carrie and Sarah rolled their eyes in response to the condescending nature of the question.

"We get many applications from students at prestigious schools, such as Illinois Math and Science Academy, Phillips Exeter Academy, and Andover, every year," the admissions rep said, deflecting the implication about New Baden beautifully. "So we're quite used to evaluating those."

"How do you take account of the fact that a place like Exeter uses the Harkness philosophy of instruction, while places such as, say, New Baden use traditional methods of instruction?" The question came from an even more well-dressed parent sitting in the first row and made the man from New Baden wince.

"Really, we don't. We look at board scores, grades based on our knowledge of a school's grading policies, teacher recommendations, extracurricular activities, and the past performance at Chicago of students from the same high school when we make the admissions decision."

"What is the average SAT of the students you accept?" The question came from a parent way in the back.

"I really don't have that statistic handy, but I can tell you that for the class that entered this fall, the median score on the SAT reasoning test was about 1,400."

The parent looked at his daughter in the next chair, who looked back at him apologetically.

"What's the lowest SAT score you will accept?" the same parent asked with great dismay.

"There is no absolute minimum number, because we look at the student's entire profile. But you can find the range for the current freshmen on our Web site."

The parent looked at his daughter again, disappointedly.

"Is it really true that this is where fun comes to die?" a very serious parent inquired. His son, who was seated next to him, rolled his eyes for all in the room to see.

The man at the front of the room smiled.

"Obviously you've read the guidebooks or seen the T-shirts some of the students wear. Our undergraduates pride themselves on how hard they work. When it comes to academics, they're a very serious bunch. But they have plenty of opportunities to have fun, whether it's through intramural sports or by exploring what the city has to offer."

"I heard that this is the place where students come to die," another father, who looked like he'd missed his shift at the factory to be there, said sarcastically. "Is it true that a lot of students here commit suicide?"

"We do have students who commit suicide, just as they do at other universities. But that's because the person is depressed; it has nothing to do with Chicago."

"What is the male-female ratio among the students?" a mother asked, making her daughter grimace.

"Actually, it's about one to one for the undergraduates."

There was a brief silence in the room.

"The word is that the women on this campus are not very attractive," one of the New Baden boys behind Carrie and Sarah whispered to his friend.

"My cousin went here a few years ago and said that he had only a handful of dates over the whole four years. He claims that masturbation was invented at the University of Chicago," his friend said and snickered.

"I wonder if anyone was awarded a Nobel Prize for that?" the first boy asked, choking with laughter.

Several girls who'd overheard their conversation gave them extremely dirty looks.

"No, but they put up a statue commemorating it. The plaque says something like 'the site of the world's first self-sustaining erection,'" the second New Baden boy said.

"You idiot, that statue is on the spot of the first self-sustaining nuclear reaction."

"Around here, the one may be just as important as the other."

"You two are both totally sick," a young female behind them muttered.

The second boy from New Baden took that as a compliment. He turned slightly to face the offended female before continuing the conversation with his friend.

"I have some good news, though, Spencer," he half-whispered, "about the women on this campus."

"What's that?"

"One of them finished second in a beauty contest last year."

"What's the bad news?"

"The beauty contest was at a leper colony."

"Screw you, you stupid asshole. You couldn't even get a date with your friend here," the girl behind them spat out as she left the room.

At that point a prospective African American student raised his hand. The man running the session seemed relieved that a non-parent was finally asking a question.

"What I want to know is this; if I come here, what is the University of Chicago going to do for me?" he asked, emphasizing the word "me."

"The university is going to give you a great education, with everything from a top notch faculty to top students who will challenge you to do your best."

"But what do you do for African American students specifically?"

"Chicago has a long history of admitting minority students, years before many other universities did. We also have need-based financial aid and merit-based scholarships."

Another father raised his hand. His question had a hard edge to it.

"Your tuition is currently around $37,000 a year. Why do you charge so much?"

"Frankly, we charge it because we can, which means that you're willing to pay it due to the quality of the education your sons and daughters will receive here."

The admissions officer's answers were highly consistent with Chicago's no-nonsense attitude toward education; however, he was quite happy when he saw that there would be no more questions from this particular audience. "Matt, who is an undergraduate student here, will take you all on the tour if you follow him outside the building. Thank you and goodbye."

A tall, red-haired boy in a blue dress shirt and khaki pants led them outside. Carrie recognized him as the guide on her tour last year. Just past the doorway they came up to Frank Foster.

"Hey, Frank," Sarah said.

"I figured you applied here, Sarah, given your plans. You, too, Carrie?"

"Yup, my application is in. I just came down with Sarah for the day. We can infer then that you're considering going here?"

"Absolutely," Frank, who stood several inches taller than either girl, answered. "It's a great place with really smart people. I'm interested in studying history and possibly economics."

They found a spot in the semi-circle around Matt the tour guide as he started talking.

"OK, if you'll follow me, I'll take you up through the main quads toward the library. Then we'll go over to the student center and then swing by the athletic fields and the hospitals before returning here."

As the group wandered toward the entrance of Regenstein Library, the guide came to an abrupt halt. He pointed to a black-haired man of average height with a pleasant face who was leaving the building and walking toward them.

"That's Robert Lawrence, the Nobel Prize-winning economist," he informed those gathered around him. "He's famous for his work in macroeconomics, especially how changes in the money supply affect measures of the real economy such as output and unemployment.

"Professor Lawrence," the guide called out. "Hi, I'm Matt Harper. I'm taking a group of prospective students and their parents around the campus and wondered if you would like to say 'hello' to them."

"Hello," he responded nonchalantly.

"Dr. Lawrence, I hope to come here and test some of your theories," a very intense Asian boy said to him.

"Then I'll check them again to make sure they're right before you get here," Professor Lawrence responded with a half-smile.

"Professor, I saw that you came from the big building behind you. Is that some sort of economics research lab where they keep data and the back issues of the *Wall Street Journal* you work with?" a mother asked.

"No, that's the library. That's where the university keeps the books."

"Professor Lawrence, to what do you ascribe the great success of the Chicago School of Economics?" one of the New Baden boys asked. Many prominent economists associated with the university, such as Milton Friedman and George Stigler, were Nobel Prize winners.

"Probably to John D. Rockefeller founding the place. The character of the department goes all the way back to the beginnings of the university."

"What I want to know is where do you think the stock market is going?" a parent blurted out.

"Where is it going? I didn't know it was leaving New York," the economist responded, trying to suppress a laugh at being asked a question that research told him was virtually unanswerable. "If you'll excuse me, I have to meet someone in my office in a couple of minutes and don't want to be late."

The tour wandered on for another half hour before coming back to its starting point.

"I have a question," Carrie asked the guide as soon as she could get his attention. "What are the students here like? Are they really cutthroat?"

"No, not at all. People go out of their way to help each other. My first year, when I was taking the required math classes, I got a lot of help from this kid on my floor at Shoreland. He's a real math whiz. In return, I edited the papers he wrote for his humanities courses. He actually helped most of the kids in the house with math at one time or another. People were doing all kinds of stuff for him in return. They were taking him out to dinner. Some girls brought him cookies and candy, and one even knitted him some sweaters, she was so grateful. The house system here really fosters collegiality."

"That's useful information," Carrie said, glancing at Sarah. "I was on one of your tours last year and don't remember hearing those details. I'm visiting with my friend today. She hasn't been here before."

"Well, I hope you both decide to come here."

As Matt excused himself, Frank Foster walked over from somewhere in the background.

"What are you guys up to now?"

"We thought we would have lunch. Where do people go to eat around here? I heard it was not a great neighborhood for food."

"Honestly, I think a lot of information people have about this place is a bit dated–like what came up at the question-and-answer session. My father went here back in the 1970s, and he says things have changed quite a lot since then, both at the university and in the neighborhood. It was dicey, with some bad areas around it, at one time. But, come on, the President of the United States lives in the Hyde Park now. How bad could it be?"

"Good point."

They walked down to a strip on 55th near the lake that boasted several restaurants, picking a Thai place Frank had heard about. The food was quite good.

"Didn't see you guys at homecoming this year," Frank observed.

"Didn't make it," Sarah responded. "I was committed to getting all those applications done, and Carrie and R.E. were helping me, so we ended up working that night."

"How was it?" Carrie asked as she put a finger nail in her mouth.

"It was OK, but not as good as last year."

"That was so much fun, especially in the park after the dance. Do you remember the impersonations Merlino did of the teachers? He does a great Ms. Smith. I laughed so hard I almost had a heart attack."

"Oh yeah, that was awesome, Carrie. You should hear Merlino tell jokes after he's had a couple of beers. I swear he's the funniest man alive when he gets going."

"So tell us one of his best jokes."

"I can't. Really, they aren't suitable for young ladies." Frank felt awkward at the possibility of telling off-color jokes to girls he respected.

"Oh, come on, Frank, we've heard it all before."

"OK, you asked for it. Here's a Merlino original," he said after a brief pause. "Did you hear about the guy who was taking steroids and Viagra at the same time?"

"No, I didn't," Carrie answered.

"He can lift five hundred pounds with his penis."

Carrie looked at Sarah, who looked back at Carrie and burst out laughing. At that point, Carrie completely cracked up.

"My God, that's funny," Carrie said once she got control of herself. "Where's Merlino applying to?"

"Illinois and also Ohio State, out of a sense of geographic loyalty. Plus some private schools. What about Taylor?"

They summarized the schools R.E. was interested in.

"Are you still dating Laurie Benton?" Sarah inquired. Carrie glanced at Frank when the question was asked.

"No, that didn't last very long. At homecoming she was paying attention to a football player she'd met that night. After that, she became more and more distant until I got the official talk in early November. 'It's just not as fun as it first was, etc. . . .' A week later she was with the other guy."

He didn't seem too concerned, perhaps because the breakup had been completely predictable.

"What do you think about U. of C.?" Frank asked, changing the subject.

"Interesting, but I don't know if I'll get in," Sarah concluded.

"We all have that problem."

"Frank, you must be kidding me. Carrie and I have that problem, not you. You're as smart as my brother, and he got in here," Sarah responded firmly.

"No one's as smart as your brother, but it was nice of you to say that," Frank said.

Leaving the restaurant they walked to one of the excellent used bookstores in Hyde Park and rummaged through the history section, finding many obscure but fascinating volumes. After that they went their separate ways and to drive home.

Sarah used her mother's car on the following Monday morning. Since there was no easy way to get to Evanston from Chicago's western suburbs, on her father's advice she headed east on North Avenue, north on Central, east on Fullerton, and then north again on Cicero. In the process Sarah and Carrie cut through the Latino sections of the city's North Side, where the small stands that had once served hot dogs and hamburgers now also sold tacos and other delights from south of the border. At Wilson Avenue she got on I-94 north and exited at Dempster in the suburbs. Near the lake, which had its back up that day, she caught Sheridan and then parked in a garage at the south end of campus. The campus was rumored to be very pretty during the warm weather, with a great view of Lake Michigan, but today she was more concerned with the strong, cold winds from the north.

With little idea about where they were going, they asked a bundled-up student for directions and arrived at the appropriate building moments before the information session began. It was, again, a fairly typical sales job for that particular university. The fun started with the Q&A.

"Do you have any same-sex dorms?" a short, middle-aged woman asked.

"Yes, we do," said the presenter, a young female admissions officer who looked like she was only a few years out of college herself.

"Do you have any no-alcohol dorms?" the same woman inquired.

"Yes, we do," was the answer again.

"Do you have any dorms that are same-sex and no-alcohol?" was the woman's final question.

"Jesus, Mother, why don't you just send me to a goddamn convent?" her daughter blurted out so loud that all could hear.

The admissions person couldn't help but smile, while the mother flushed red in embarrassment as everyone else in the room laughed.

A boy at the front of the room raised his hand. "Like every other university, you make the admissions decision based on six semesters of coursework in high school. On top of that we have to submit our grades from the first semester of senior year after we apply. Are grades after that ignored?"

"No, they're not. We do look at grades during the final semester and we can rescind a decision to admit if those grades drop a lot."

"Theoretically speaking, how much would the grades have to drop for the decision to be reversed?" The speaker seemed worried.

"By a lot, theoretically speaking," she said in return, wondering how bad the questioner's spring semester grades would likely be.

"Why do you charge so much per year in tuition?" a father asked next.

"Sir, we provide only the best education for your children, and we take very good care of them while they're here. That type of quality costs money. Don't you want the finest education possible for your son or daughter?"

A hand went up in the back of the room and was acknowledged.

"In your admissions process, how do you take account of the fact that a student might be from a prestigious high school, such as New Baden, as opposed to a high school in Podunk, Ohio?" The questioner was the New Baden parent, sitting with the same adult and the two obnoxious boys, who had been in their group at Chicago the past Friday.

Sarah smiled and motioned to Carrie that she was going out in the hallway. Carrie grabbed her coat off the back of the chair and followed her.

"No more of that, thank you very much," Sarah said.

"Yes, it gets old," Carrie added.

"Are these two sessions that I've been at pretty typical?"

"I would say so, although the questions have been a bit more off the wall than I remember."

"So I was right in not wanting to make campus visits?"

"They're not worthless, but they're not always that informative either. I would say you have to extract a lot of rock and dirt from the mine to get at the gold."

Carrie and Sarah hung out in the hallway until it was time for the tour. The young woman who suffered through the questions led those assembled out of the room and out the door. Because of the fierce wind, the group frequently huddled on the south side of buildings so that they could hear her commentary. She pointed out various edifices on campus, which were a mix of architectural styles, in terms of their functions and their history. In the shelter of Leverone Hall, the main building of the Kellogg School of Business, their guide noticed two elderly gentlemen walking toward the group.

"Here comes Professor Hochstattler, the Nobel laureate in physics, and his colleague Professor Darmstadt," she said in an excited tone.

"Do the senior faculty here teach undergraduate courses?" a young Indian prospect asked.

"Yes, they love to teach undergraduates!"

As the physicists approached, the tour guide called out to them cheerfully.

"Professor Hochstattler! Professor Darmstadt! This is a group of prospective undergraduate students and their parents," she said, moving her hand with a flourish in the direction of those she was leading.

"Really?" Hochstattler responded, drawing his head back to survey the people standing before him with curiosity. "So that's what they look like? Lord knows I haven't taught an undergraduate course in thirty-five years."

"Some of them look very young. Don't they, Dieter?" Professor Darmstadt asked.

"They're supposed to. Undergraduates are young."

"But these other ones don't appear to be young at all."

"The other ones are the parents," Professor Hochstattler pointed out to Darmstadt, who was a theoretical physicist.

"Will you be teaching undergraduates in the near future, Professor

Hochstattler?" the young woman asked, trying to recover some credibility with her tour group.

"Certainly not. Young lady, I did not win the Nobel Prize for teaching. I won it for my research," Hochstattler sniffed.

The admissions officer was seemingly intent on digging an even a deeper hole for herself, so she opened her mouth again.

"But you employ advanced undergraduates in your labs to help you with research, don't you?" she pleaded.

"Of course not," Darmstadt responded. "You think we want to let them blow the bloody place up?"

"Come, Friedrich," Hochstattler said matter of factly. "They're having Wiener schnitzel for lunch at the faculty club, and we don't want to be late. There's nothing worse than tepid sauerkraut."

As the physicists strolled off, the tour group members looked at each other skeptically. The admissions officer was rather taciturn during the rest of the tour and unloaded her group as soon as she could. Carrie and Sarah then wandered into downtown Evanston and found a Starbucks. Sarah, who was now permanently allergic to coffee, bought a cup of tea while Carrie ordered a latte. The hot beverages helped them warm up.

"Damn, I feel sorry for the woman from the admissions office. Running into Goering and Himmler like that could not have been any worse than it was," Sarah said. "Do you think that after lunch they'll invade Poland?"

"I'm sure that all the faculty at Northwestern are not like that," Carrie offered, trying to draw broader conclusions from the encounter. "But frankly the message you hear around the country is that at many of the best universities the top faculty don't teach undergraduates."

"So what do they do?"

"I guess they teach graduate students and work closely with them, including on dissertations."

"So?"

"That impacts the faculty members' research."

"So what?"

"And it affects the research of the graduate students."

"So, what good is that to us?"

"Not a lot, at least not directly," Carries responded, scratching the back of her head. "But if it raises the quality of the department and the prestige of the university, it attracts better junior faculty, who will teach our courses, and better students for us to be around."

"Whatever," Sarah said in frustration. "I don't see where we're going to get a lot out of guys like those two."

They fled the Starbucks as the New Baden parents and their offspring entered. After browsing the stacks of the library to see what the university held in certain areas, Carrie sensed that Sarah was bored with it all, so they poked around Evanston rather than exploring Northwestern further. After a late lunch at a burger place, they drove home in an attempt to beat the traffic on the Edens Expressway.

R.E., cupcakes in hand, came by that night to go over some material in AP Euro with Sarah, and she shared the experiences of the last few days with him. He laughed at the stories from the question-and-answer sessions.

"It's not so bad, Sarah. Even if you didn't learn a ton, at least you got out and had some fun with Carrie."

"Actually, I think Carrie learned more than I did," Sarah commented.

Sarah was in a buoyant mood, having received letters the last few days from a number of schools admitting her in the fall. She showed them to R.E.

"Sarah, I don't mean to rain on your parade, but these are all places lower on your list. If you go online, you'll see that in the last cycle some of them accepted over fifty percent of the applicants. We're not talking Harvard, Stanford, or Yale here in terms of how selective some of these places are."

"I know. I still haven't heard from the really top schools," she said wearily.

"All truth will be revealed in about a month," R.E. reminded her. "In meantime, have a cupcake."

The next four weeks dragged on as Carrie, R.E., Sarah, and many high school seniors around the country waited to hear from the remaining schools on their lists. The three of them whiled away the time, keeping their mind off of the process, by exploring the city–something they had started doing the summer after their junior year. It was fun to get out of Oak Stream and wander around Chicago's ethnic neighborhoods, eat at different restaurants, and visit its cultural institutions.

The associate dean at Washington University was right in one respect; as more and more schools learned that Harvard and Stanford were admitting Sarah, they put her application in the admit pile–with one exception.

Late one day a junior admissions officer at the University of Chicago was still working after many of his colleagues had gone home. A stack of applications from local students sat under his desk lamp. These were the last ones that he needed to make a decision on before a more senior person reviewed his recommendations. On his way out, the dean of undergraduate students walked past and stopped by the open door.

"Working late, Charlie?"

"Yes, Dean Barnard. I'm wrestling with the last of these."

"Any problems?"

"There's this one here. Sarah Jennings, the girl in all the newspaper articles. She's a very good student, in about the top five percent of her graduating class, and she has some strong letters of recommendation plus a creative essay. But there's nothing really extraordinary here. On the other hand, the word is that Harvard, Stanford, and most everyone else is admitting her because she's famous."

"So what? Let them. This is Chicago. We don't do that here," the dean responded. "Who else have you got there?"

"There's this girl from the same high school, similar academically and in terms of letters of recommendation, but she has better extracurricular activities. Second team all state in lacrosse and team captain and all sectional in Scholastic Bowl." He pointed at a folder labeled "Caroline Wilson."

"Admit her instead because she has the stronger package, and call it a night. You look like you could use some rest. Sometimes I think this process is harder on us than it is on the high school students," the dean observed.

Elsewhere in the country that evening, a young admissions person named Robert Burns was also working late. He had a stack of applications from the Midwest on his desk, all from Illinois, trying to determine how many would be admitted given the university's desired geographical mix for the entering class. As he glanced at one folder, he felt that his eyes were playing tricks on him. He blinked several times and then examined it again. The page in front of him seemed familiar. Quickly he shuffled through the pile of folders and found what he wanted somewhere near the middle. He laid two folders side by side and compared the contents. His suspicions confirmed, he sent his boss, Associate Dean Jennifer Logan, an e-mail asking to see her right away the next morning.

At 8:30 a.m. Burns walked into his superior's office and sat down. She was in an extremely foul mood. Exhausted after several long weeks of combing through freshman applications, it made her contemplate how much longer she wanted to stay in this job that, in her opinion, did not pay handsomely.

"So, Robert?" she asked.

"Jennifer, I was going through the applications from Illinois last night and I noticed something really peculiar. A minority application accidentally got into the pile I had of Caucasian applications."

She gave him a blank stare.

"The minority application is from a Running Elk Taylor who attends Oak Stream High School outside of Chicago. It looked familiar so I dug out another application, from Robert E. Taylor, also at Oak Stream. It's the same application–exactly the same courses, the exact same grades. The essays and letters of recommendation are also verbatim identical. If it would have been in the right group, I would never have noticed it."

"Could they be identical twins?" his superior asked, furrowing her brow in an attempt at deep thought.

"No. It's the same social security number. With absolute certainty the same guy has applied here twice, once as a Native American and once as a Caucasian."

Jennifer Logan pondered the situation for a few moments.

"Tell me about the application."

"He's a very good but not exceptional student. He's in roughly the top five percent of his class and top five percent on the SAT. What stands out is his work in the field of history."

"So accept this one," she said pointing at the application from Running Elk Taylor, "and reject that one. We don't really need any more male Caucasians from the Midwest this year."

"You're serious?" Burns asked with disbelief, not quite sure whether he heard her correctly and wanting a more senior person to take full responsibility for this particular decision.

"Yes, I'm completely goddamn serious!"

Robert Burns stiffened in his chair.

"You've been in this job long enough to know how it works. You've got your piles to deal with and I have mine." She gestured toward an imaginary pile of folders on her clean desk. "First there's this pile I have to worry about. Those are the athletes. Since we compete in Division I, we probably let in three hundred people a year–even though most of them won't come here–to keep the men's and women's programs well stocked in all the sports. Then there's this other pile containing all the young Mozarts, Rembrandts, Einsteins, Isaac Newtons, and Rockefellers who already have notable achievements in music, art, science, math, or business even though they are still in high school. We absolutely have to admit them–even though we, despite our very high opinion of ourselves as a university, are nothing but their safety school and they are almost certainly all going to Harvard or Stanford because, in their minds, and those of their parents, they are somehow better places."

Jennifer Logan came up briefly for air before continuing.

"Then there's this pile. See how big this one is? These are the legacies and other applicants with pull. Such as the children of multimillionaires whom the development office has been courting for God only knows how long. Or the offspring of really connected people. Even though many of them don't belong here because they can't handle the coursework, these kids or their parents have decided they want to go here and sadly they will come here if we admit them. Do you know what happens if I don't accept one of them? Five minutes after they get the letter, the dean will be ripping me a new one in my office because he just got ripped one over the phone. Then we have the smallest pile. The quality minority applications. Do you know how hard it is to find academically strong Native American applicants, given where we are located? This Taylor kid scored well on the SAT. We are absolutely going to admit him, regardless of anything else we know about him, and I'm going to recommend that he gets a free ride. A full scholarship for all four years. If he comes here, the dean is likely to walk into my office and pat me on the head or give me some other completely meaningless sign of gratitude because I conjured up a strong Native American kid."

"But even though the pile of quality minority applicants is small, that doesn't mean that we won't be admitting lots of minorities. So another large block of those admitted, given that we accept X people a year, is spoken for. Then what's left? The massive pile of ordinary applicants, such as Caucasian kids without exemplary qualities, of whom we can only admit a fairly small number. Including kids from the Midwest who are not overly likely to come here anyway because when push comes to shove they decide not to go too far away from Des Moines or Terre Haute or Hooterville or wherever the hell they're from because they can't stand the idea of leaving the cornfields behind. So how in God's name do you expect me to admit this Robert E. Taylor when we have a large pile of fiercely competitive similar applications from the Midwest for a handful of spots?"

Robert Burns walked out of that office and thought long and hard about whether he should go back to school to get a master's degree and find a new line of work sooner rather than later.

Back in Oak Stream that evening, while she sat on her bed reading, Sarah's cell phone rang. She grabbed it off the desk. Looking at the number, she saw that it was her brother calling.

"Hey, Ben," she said eagerly.

"Hi, Sarah. I'm calling to see how you're doing."

"I'm just sitting and waiting. I should hear from the remaining colleges in a couple more days."

"That's partly what I'm calling you about," Ben said, taking a deep breath. "The dean of undergraduates here at Harvard called me personally to let me know, and he said it was OK to tell you, that you've been accepted by Harvard. Congratulations, Sarah, your strategy is paying off."

"Wow, are you serious?" she gasped.

"Yes, I'm totally serious. Not only did they want me to tell you, but I'm also supposed to convince you to come here."

"Really? Oh, I don't know, Ben. Harvard is for people like you. All the kids at Oak Stream say that you are the smartest kid they've ever met."

"Sarah, Harvard is a great place. Don't make any mistake about that. But not everyone, and I'm not trying to sound conceited, is just like me. There are lots of kids, if you look at their academic records, who are very similar to you or not as strong as you. They just happen to be the son or daughter of a governor or an ambassador or something like that. I know that for a fact because when I first got here I was worried about how tough the competition might be, so I asked most of the people I met about their backgrounds. Plus, I'll be here to help you, if you need or want it, your first two years as an undergraduate."

Sarah thought for a moment.

"Where else have you heard from?" Ben asked.

"I've gotten letters from a lot of the state schools on my list but not too many of the private ones because they don't have rolling admissions." She ticked off the names of a few of her acceptances.

"Those are some good places and I suspect you'll get some good news from other schools too." He said it so slyly that Sarah wondered whether he knew more than he was telling her.

Ben informed her that Harvard was willing to pay her plane fare to Boston if she would come out for several days to visit the campus.

"I'll find girls in my dorm you can stay with, so all you'll need is money for meals, at least when Harvard is not picking those up. You can sit in on my classes and talk to some of the faculty members. I've already spoken to them about it and they would like you to contact them if you have any questions."

Sarah told Ben that she would think about it and get back to him.

10
DECISIONS, DECISIONS

At the beginning of April, they received the last of the letters determining their fate. Sarah gleefully read them, finding herself accepted by one university after another. It was like opening an endless pile of presents on Christmas morning.

Carrie and R.E. had mixed results. They met at Sarah's one Wednesday to go over the news.

"Here's the bottom line, you guys. I got accepted everywhere I applied to, excluding Chicago and Wash. U."

"Those two rejected you? No accounting for taste I guess," Carrie concluded.

"Wow, you're ninety-nine and two, Sarah," R.E. said with a smile.

"I don't know how that happened. So many of those were reach schools for me," Sarah stated.

Both Carrie and R.E. quietly attributed it to her notoriety.

"Come on, give it up, guys. What about you?' Sarah asked in return.

"I'm five for eleven," Carrie summarized. "Got accepted by Michigan and Illinois, as you know, plus Chicago, MIT, and Berkeley and rejected by Yale, Princeton, Stanford, Columbia, and Hopkins."

"R.E.?"

R.E. seemed a little out of sorts.

"Running Elk Taylor was accepted by Yale, Berkeley, Princeton, Harvard, Stanford, Columbia, Hopkins, Michigan, and Illinois. He has been offered sizable grants or scholarships by all four Ivy League schools and also Stanford and Hopkins. In fact, he has received extremely nice letters from very high level people at each school, beseeching him to matriculate because he will be a valuable addition to the school's student body and will further himself immensely by attending said school. Numerous phone calls have been received from current students, alumni, and university staffers reiterating how happy each school would be if Running Elk Taylor would be so kind as to attend said school. On the other hand, Robert Edward Taylor was accepted by the U. of I. and rejected by the other eight."

"That's great. We all have great choices," Sarah said, happy for both her friends.

Carrie smiled a little nervously while R.E. did not.

Sarah received a call the next day from Page Brooks, who was gathering information for a follow-up story. Page seemed more interested in where Sarah was accepted than in her own college choices.

A few days later the *Sentinel* ran as their top story an article entitled "The Girl Who Was Accepted (Almost) Everywhere."

For Sarah Jennings it will soon be 'Good-bye, Oak Stream' and 'Hello, Guinness Book of World Records.' Like the rest of the seniors around the country, she has received all her college acceptance or rejection letters at this point. Of the 101 universities she applied to, she was accepted by all of them—except for Chicago and Washington University in St. Louis. That's right, 99 acceptances and only two rejections. She has been admitted by such stellar institutions as Harvard, Princeton, Yale, MIT, Stanford, Cal Tech, Penn, Columbia, and Duke, to name just a few.

"Both the 101 applications and the 99 acceptances overall, much less from almost all the top schools in the country, are surely records," Ms. Smith from the history division commented. Several staff members and administrators, speaking to the Sentinel on the condition of anonymity, were quite surprised by the schools that admitted her.

"Sarah is a very good student," one teacher said, "but a number of these were long shots for her because they are deluged with applications from very good students. I'm amazed she got into so many of the ones on the very top of her list."

"There is an important lesson here about the process for other high school students," a guidance counselor observed. "The decisions made by colleges are sometimes almost arbitrary, and students should not be overly concerned about what any particular school decides. Why was she admitted by these 99, but those two rejected her?"

The article went on to speculate about where Sarah might matriculate, based on the places her friends or other top Oak Stream students were admitted to, including a roundup of which Ivy League and other elite institutions the valedictorians would be attending in the fall. It was a nice segueway from Sarah to the senior class in general and the remaining problem of choosing a university after getting admitted.

Not long after this, Sarah started to hear from the relatives again. Although she was not aware of it, her parents had absolutely forbidden anyone outside of her two brothers to speak to her about colleges while she was applying or waiting for the decisions. It was a Herculean effort by them. But once they knew which universities accepted her, the relatives asked her parents if they could call under the guise of offering their congratulations.

The first time her cell phone rang it was her uncle Joe.

"Hi, Uncle Joe," she said nonchalantly.

"Hi, Sarah. Is what I heard from your parents true? You've been accepted to all eight Ivy League schools?"

"Yes, along with a number of others," she responded.

"That's great. You can't go wrong there. I'm so very proud of you. I wonder how many people got into all eight Ivies?"

"I don't know, Uncle Joe. They're really good schools, and I'm sure lots of people besides me would like to go there."

"Sarah, don't listen to your uncle," her aunt Stephanie said from another phone in their place in Manhattan. "If I can offer a little bit of advice, I think you should go to a good school, and there are lots of them, just not one in the Midwest. Get out and see the world. Plus, you will meet boys who are so much more *sophisticated* than those in the Midwest." The word "sophisticated" did a pirouette off her tongue.

Sarah stopped to reflect whether the few boys she had been on dates with were sophisticated or not.

"So I should meet boys who are sophisticated? I'll write that down," she answered, pretending to write on a pad of paper on her desk.

"Sarah, don't worry right now about what your aunt says. Get the best education you can. You can always work in New York City later, where there will be no shortage of interesting young men. The doors of New York City will be wide open for you after you finish at an Ivy League school."

"I've got that written down here. Thanks for calling, but I really have to go."

The same night the Defender of the Faith, her Grandma Mary, called. "Sarah, I spoke to your parents and they told me about all the schools that accepted you. I just wanted to know, are any of them Catholic institutions?"

"Yes, Grandma, I think six of them are."

"Which ones, honey?"

"Notre Dame, Georgetown, Boston College, Fordham, Marquette, and St. Louis University."

"Those are the only ones on that whole list of top schools with a religious affiliation when there are so many fine Catholic universities out there?"

"Gee, no, Grandma. I was also accepted at Brandeis and Yeshiva University," Sarah said, throwing her a curve.

"But, dear, those aren't Catholic schools."

"Oh, I'm sorry, Grandma. I must have misheard you. What about Ohio State, where they worship the football team?"

"That's not an organized religion, Sarah, much less the Catholic religion."

"I'd say it's fairly organized, Grandma. The football team practices more times a week than most of the Christian faiths and some of their followers border on the fanatical," Sarah teased. "But OK, we'll skip Ohio State then. Do you really think I should go to a Catholic university?"

"Yes, I think it would be very good for you. You'll get a religious based education with a firm set of values."

"I'm going to write that down, Grandma, on this pad of paper on my desk so that I don't forget," Sarah informed her without picking up a pen or pencil.

A week later Carrie and R.E. were slumped in Sarah's room, listening to Sarah complain about her relatives and sharing gossip about where their classmates were admitted and who was leaning which way.

"What about us? Is there any chance at all that we might end up at the same place?" Sarah asked.

"Running Elk Taylor," he intoned strangely, "and the two of you have been admitted to Illinois, Michigan, and Berkeley. So it would have to be one of those three. That assumes, of course, that Carrie will not be going to MIT."

"Actually, guys, I've made up my mind and was going to tell you tonight, at least with regard to MIT. I decided it's too damn cutthroat. I would just hate it there," Carrie said almost apologetically. "It's going to be one of the other four–the three you just mentioned or Chicago."

"Wow. Have you told your parents yet? What will they say?" Sarah asked with concern.

"No, I haven't told them yet. I need more time. But you know what? I don't care if they don't like it. I'm done worrying about what they or my mother, to be more specific, want." She bit off a fingernail.

"Why not just tell them now?" R.E. asked, trying to be helpful.

"Because I have to decide which place I'm actually going to, so that I can give them the wonderful news all at once?" Carrie's raised voice bounced off the walls of the room. "Plus I need time to pile sandbags around myself as protection against the shrapnel that will be coming at me from all directions when my mother learns that I'm not going to MIT!"

"Good luck, Carrie. I know you'll make the right decision," Sarah added quickly, trying to move the conversation elsewhere.

"Thanks," she responded in a soft voice as she looked at Sarah.

"What about you, Sarah? Have you decided?" R.E. asked.

"I don't know now that I have to choose between ninety-nine top schools," she said and sighed.

"You have to make a decision soon; you don't have much time."

"I know, but it's so hard," Sarah pleaded.

"Sarah, have you ever heard the saying 'Don't wish too hard for something because you might get it?'" R.E. asked.

Before Sarah could answer, Carrie completely blew up.

"You know, Running Elk, just because you got into every place you applied to and probably have already decided, it doesn't mean that you can be condescending to us! I have a question for you; are you completely unable to keep your mouth shut?" She grabbed her coat and put it on.

"Sarah, I have to go. Good night," Carrie said and walked out the door.

"What the heck was that all about?" R.E. asked defensively a bit later.

"Her mother will give her holy hell for turning down MIT. I doubt if you understand how determined she is that Carrie goes there and how domineering she can be."

He hung his head dejectedly. "I knew her mother had some loyalty to the place, but I didn't think it was that bad. I'll apologize when I see Carrie tomorrow," R.E. offered. "To tell you the truth, Sarah, I haven't decided yet, but I'm leaning in a particular direction. I'll let you know when my mind is made up. This really hasn't been easy for me, despite what Carrie thinks."

"It certainly isn't easy for me, either. I never thought that I would find myself in this position. I figured that out of the top fifty on my list, maybe ten or twenty would admit me, beyond Illinois. Throw in some more from the last fifty, and it's a small set I could wade through, especially if I focused on the top places. Since I couldn't decide on which school I wanted, I was going to let them largely decide for me. How did I know that almost everyone would accept me?"

"What do you think you'll do?"

"I'm going to see Ms. Smith tomorrow and get her advice."

The next afternoon Sarah and Ms. Smith sat in her classroom.

"I've been admitted to all these places, but I have no idea how to decide among them."

Ms. Smith crossed her legs and adjusted her skirt.

"Sarah, you're in the same predicament as the dog that chased the garbage truck. Once it caught the truck, the dog couldn't figure out what to do with it. By not trimming down the schools you were interested in before applying, you didn't solve the problem; you merely delayed it and made it much more difficult. I tried to warn you about this at the beginning of the year when you came to see me, but you had the 'bit in your teeth,' as they say in horse racing. When that happens you can't stop the horse from running."

Her critical remarks reminded Sarah so much of R.E.'s comment about wishing too hard for something, but she took no offense. "So what do I do now?"

"I suggest that you start by doing triage on the schools you've been admitted to." In response to Sarah's quizzical look she continued. "It's a technique that was used by French battlefield doctors in World War I. Wounded soldiers reaching the aid station were divided into three groups: those whom medical assistance would probably not help, those whom medical attention would probably help, and those who would probably be fine without medical assistance. Divide your schools into three categories: those you really want to attend, those you might want to attend and those you don't want to attend. In a group that large, there will surely be a number you can put in the last category."

"OK."

"After that you can do a further cut to get it down to what you might call semi-finalists, then another cut to get the finalists, and eventually you pick one. That's basically the process that is used when there are many applicants for a job. The committee evaluating the applications whittles the pool down in stages."

"Ms. Smith, thank you. I'll get started on the triage tonight."

She called Carrie and R.E., who were on speaking terms again, and asked them to come over.

"Guys, we're going to go through the *U. S. News and World Report* list I printed out a while ago and do triage on the ninety-nine remaining schools. Carrie, if you'll grab that red pen from my desk and read the names, I would appreciate it. R.E., I would like you to sit by my computer, in case we need to google them to do follow-up research. I'll give each school a number from one to three or say 'Pass.' A '1' means I'm interested, a '2' means I may be interested, and a '3' means I'm not interested and the school is out for good. If I say 'Pass' we'll come back to it. Carrie, please write the numbers down, including a '3' for Chicago and Wash. U. since they didn't admit me."

After several runs through the list every school was in one of three groups. Some of the decisions were incredibly easy. She rejected MIT on the same grounds as Carrie. A few schools were dropped because they had a technological bent, such as Cal Tech and Stevens Institute of Technology, or did not seem to be focused on the liberal arts, such as SUNY College of Environmental Science and Forestry. Any school with a hardcore party reputation joined them. Other decisions were more difficult. In numerous cases she rejected schools based on fairly arbitrary impressions about how prestigious they were or how strong their history department was.

When it was all said and done, three very painful hours had gone by—replete with frustration and angst—but 37 of the 99 universities that had admitted her were no longer under consideration.

Unfortunately, 62 were still in the picture. She thanked Carrie and R.E. for their time but felt no better than before. Her request for advice from them on which university to attend was met with an answer similar to those she had heard many times before; "Only you can make that decision, Sarah."

She pondered the list for several days before going to see Ms. Smith again.

"I did the triage, which was really hard because I don't know a lot about most of these places, so it seems very arbitrary to summarily dismiss them. Regardless of that my list is still really long. Many of them are prestigious schools, to use the word everyone else uses to describe them, so I don't feel like I'm any closer to a decision," she confessed to Ms. Smith in her room.

"Sarah, don't worry about prestige, which is largely someone else's perception of something. Find the place that's right for you."

"How do I do that?"

"You took AP economics, right? In economic analysis, how do people make decisions? Based on someone else's tastes? By buying the most expensive item available? Or based on what's available, the cost of what is available, their own financial resources, and their tastes?"

"The latter," she responded.

"Sarah, you need to sit down and be very introspective and think about what you want, given the position you're in."

"That makes sense. I've focused on the schools the whole time, rather than on myself and my circumstances." Sarah reflected for a moment. "One other thing from Mr. Porter's AP econ class is obvious to me now, too."

"What's that?"

"The idea that people don't like uncertainty," Sarah answered with a pretend frown.

In the halls of the high school at the same time, near R.E.'s locker, Tim Tyler was complaining loudly to his friends.

"God damn it! I lost my three-ring binder with all my notes in it. I'm totally and irrevocably screwed. I'll never make it through my classes, and Illinois will revoke my football scholarship."

"You had all your notes in one binder?" a friend of his asked.

"Yes, I write them on loose-leaf, hole-punched paper and then put them in a binder so they're all in one place."

"Can't you just get someone else's notes from each class?"

"No, that won't work for me. I got some class notes from other people when I was a sophomore and they didn't help me. I can only study from the ones I take."

Incapable of tears, Tyler was at that moment quite capable of killing someone. R.E., who heard every word, recognized that he was in a very unique position.

"Hey, Tyler," R.E. called to him.

"*What?*" the football player responded with a malicious stare. He started toward R.E., his massive hands coming up from his sides.

"Were they in a dark green binder, with some writing on the front in black marker?"

"Yeah, did you see it?"

"I found it under a chair in the library. I turned it in to the front desk there last period."

Tim Tyler turned and, without saying another word, ran at full speed toward the library. Groups of people in the hall scattered toward the lockers to avoid being trampled.

R.E. left school a few minutes later and started to walk home. When he was a block away Tim Tyler ran up behind him, causing him to turn suddenly.

"Hey, Taylor. Look, I know we haven't been very friendly to each other going all the way back to the start of freshman year. I also know you didn't have to tell me where my notebook was. You could just not have said anything about it and let me sink. But you saved my ass. I owe you, man. I owe you big time. Friends?" Tim Tyler offered, stretching out a huge hand.

"OK," he said, shaking it.

"If I can ever do anything for you, dude, just let me know."

When Sarah got home, she shot up to her bedroom to tackle the college decision again. Instead of staring at the list of 62 schools, she sat with her eyes closed and thought about things. She'd stuck the list in a desk drawer so that she would not have to see it.

After an hour Sarah went down to the kitchen where her mother was watching the small television mounted above the counter top while emptying the dishwasher.

"Got a second, Mom?"

"Sure," she said as she put away the glasses.

"I'm having trouble now deciding on which college to go to."

"I'm not at all surprised. You have so many choices. Are you going to visit Harvard?"

"I don't think so. It's nice of them to offer to fly me out and everything, but there just isn't enough time. I do need your help, though. Do you have any motherly advice for me?"

Mrs. Jennings put down a glass and a dish towel as she thought for a moment. "Sarah, the first thing you need to realize is that it's not you. This is really hard. Step back and think about it for a minute. This is the first time you—or most people your age—have been forced to make a major decision by yourself. Up until now, everything important had been decided for you. Where Dad and I chose to live determined what schools you went to, after we, not you, made the decision to send you to the public schools. Can you name even one major decision you've had to make?"

"What color Ipod to get?" Sarah asked with a grin.

"Exactly. You get my point," her mother said, turning off the television. "The college application process is the start of a major change in your life. From now on the big decisions are all up to you. There will be a number of them over the next few years alone, and they all have one thing in common. In each one, you are making a major decision with only very limited information."

"Not sure I completely follow you, Mom," Sarah responded. Based on the number of guidebooks and such, it seemed to her that there was an almost infinite amount of information available about the various universities. More information than anyone could possibly absorb.

"You don't have anywhere near perfect information about these different schools, so you're making a decision largely in the dark. It doesn't matter how many books, college brochures, or Web sites you've looked at or how many people you talk to who went there. There is no way you can find out, unless you go there, if a particular place is right for you. The same thing will happen to you over and over again in life. You'll pick a graduate school, take a job, change jobs, choose a place to live, marry a guy, buy a house, vote for politicians, make decisions for your kids, on and on and on, all without perfect information."

Mrs. Jennings paused and reflected back on her own life.

"But you know what? The good news is that even though you don't know and can't know everything when you pick a college, it will most likely work out all right. Why? Because there are lots of good schools out there, all of which are able to give most kids the classes they need. But your education is largely what you make of it. If you go there to work hard, you can get a good education at most places." She paused again.

"If you don't believe me, think about the millions of high school kids before you who went through exactly the same process, flying largely in the dark when choosing a college, and it all worked out. Just like your choice of graduate school, career, job, spouse, and house will work out if you work at it. And, once you make a major decision like this and it works out, all the ones after this will be easier."

"Mom, wow. Thank you. That makes me feel so much better," Sarah said in gratitude. "It doesn't necessarily help me make the decision, but it makes me feel good about whatever decision I make. Also, I want to thank you and Dad for not continually bothering me about this. You've been great."

"Sarah, we just want what's best for you," her mother said, kissing her softly on the forehead.

"By the way, Mom, why did you choose Notre Dame?" she asked earnestly.

"Because it was close to home. It allowed me to commute and work about twenty hours a week at a department store in South Bend that paid fairly well. I don't think we could have afforded it otherwise. Plus, I was able to help out on the farm at crunch times."

"What about the rest of your family?"

"My brothers Bill and Chuck were the only ones of my siblings to go to college. They went to Indiana because Notre Dame really did not have strong programs in the areas they wanted to study and it was low cost. Plus it wasn't so far away that they couldn't come home on weekends as necessary."

"So they used pretty much the same reasoning as you. They just ended up at a different place."

"I guess that's right," her mother answered. "Why don't you ask your father the same question?"

"I will after dinner."

A few hours later the dinner dishes had been cleared, and everyone had gone to their separate corners of the house.

"Dad," Sarah asked, joining her father in the study, "I've asked Mom this question already. How did you end up at Brown?"

"It was pretty simple really. They offered me some significant money, it was very strong in the social sciences, and I wanted a place with small class sizes."

"What about Uncle Joe and Uncle Bob?" she continued.

"Your uncle Bob went to Indiana."

"Why Indiana?"

"Bob was a hell of a basketball player in high school. Indiana under Bobby Knight offered him a full scholarship. So did Illinois by the way, but Indiana had a better business school and a better basketball program, so it was straightforward for him."

"I didn't know that Uncle Bob played basketball," Sarah gasped. It was one of her favorite sports.

"He hasn't played in a long time. He blew out his knee really bad during a game, I think when he was a sophomore, and has not really played since. Back then it was nowhere near as easy to recover from that kind of injury as it is today. I think he was not interested in playing pick-up or rec league basketball after college, so you've probably never heard him talk about playing anywhere."

"What about Uncle Joe?"

"Your uncle Joe went to Illinois and studied business."

"He didn't go to an Ivy League school?" Sarah asked in disbelief.

"He applied to a few, partly because I was already at Brown, but he didn't get admitted. I'm sure he would have done fine there, but it was hard to get into the Ivies, even back then. Illinois he got into, along with Northwestern and some smaller private schools in the Midwest plus some state schools. I think Oberlin, Macalester, and maybe Michigan and Ohio State accepted him."

"But every time he talks to me about this stuff, it's Ivy League this and Ivy League that."

Her father laughed softly. "Your uncle Joe came to love the Ivy League after he went to Wall Street. Unless you know someone, the investment banks will hire undergraduates from only a handful of schools. That's the only part of higher education my brother Joe cares to see. When he had to choose, he wanted to go into accounting. The private schools he got into did not really have business programs at the undergraduate level, and at Michigan and Ohio State it would have been a lot more expensive than Illinois and not necessarily better. The decision really made itself."

"What about Aunt Stephanie? Did she go to the Sorbonne or some place like that?"

Her father laughed out loud for what seemed like 30 seconds at that one. "Your uncle met your aunt at Illinois. She was in a sorority that his fraternity was close to," he said with a bit of a 'let me set you straight' tone. "She's from the northern suburbs of Chicago originally. All that affectation comes from Uncle Joe's success on Wall Street and the big money he gets by working an ungodly number of hours a week. She dressed nicely, even in college, but otherwise she was pretty much like everyone else."

"What about the rest of your family?"

"Your aunt Susan went to Illinois also, like my brother Joe because the price was right. In terms of your grandparents, Grandma Mary went to Rosary College, which is not too far from here. It's called Dominican now."

"Why did she go there?"

"In the old days there were various Catholic women's colleges around the Chicago area. Families tended to cloister the girls a bit until they got married, so no public schools or colleges far away from home for them. Rosary was the place for really smart Catholic girls, and her family offered to pay for her education if she went there."

"And no money if she went somewhere else?"

"Nope, just for Rosary."

"That's pretty old school, isn't it?"

"Yes, that's the way they did it back then."

Sarah understood her paternal grandmother a little better at this point.

"What about Grandpa? Did he go to college?"

"Yes, to a small liberal arts college out East. When he came home after World War II, the veterans received college education under the G.I. Bill. His base was near there, and that's where they sent him."

"Hmm, that's interesting," Sarah murmured.

She thanked her father for his input and went up to her room.

There was a text from Carrie on her cell phone asking if it was OK to come over. She also wanted R.E. to be there. Sarah also had messages from Page Brooks and some newspaper reporters, wondering whether she had made a decision. She ignored those for the time being.

When Carrie arrived, she looked like she was ready to burst from all the pressure she was under. Glancing at Sarah, who was seated on the bed, and R.E., who was sitting in the desk chair turned backwards, she cleared her throat.

"I've decided. I'm going to Chicago."

"Congratulations, Carrie," Sarah said, rising to give her a hug. The two girls embraced for almost a minute, and then R.E. hugged Carrie as well.

"What made you pick Chicago?"

"It's obviously a really good university, but I think it was what the tour guide said when we were there—that kids really watch each others' backs. The house system seems to foster that."

"Have you told your parents?" Sarah asked.

"No, I'm going to wait until the appropriate time."

"Since we're all together, I think I should tell you both that I've reached a decision."

"Where is it going to be, R.E.?" Carrie asked.

"I don't want to say anything right now, but you'll know soon. I have my reasons," he said, giving no further hints about what was going on.

They and everyone else at Oak Stream read about his decision a few days later in an op-ed piece in the *Chicago Tribune*.

A Tale of Two Taylors

My name is Taylor. I was born Robert Edward (aka Rob) Taylor and am one-eighth Potawatomi. I am a senior at Oak Stream High School and applied to nine universities this year under that name, listing my ethnicity as Caucasian. Many of these are very prestigious schools, such as Harvard, Princeton, and Stanford. After those applications were submitted, I legally changed my name to Running Elk Taylor and applied again to the same nine schools. Each application was verbatim identical to the one previously submitted—same letters of recommendation, same transcripts, same essays, same social security number, etc.—except for my name and the fact that I checked the box for Native American.

Robert Edward Taylor was admitted by just the University of Illinois at Urbana-Champaign. Running Elk Taylor, on the other hand, was admitted by all nine schools and in some cases was offered grants and scholarships (which need not be repaid, as opposed to loans) to attend.

What caused this rather dichotomous behavior on the part of some of America's finest universities? I have spent quite a bit of time thinking about that. It could be inexactness in the admissions process, such as two different evaluators reading the "different" files, just as you might get different advice on how to do your taxes if you take them to different preparers. After all, I'm a good student but not a brilliant one by modern standards, so my application would surely be in the gray area. But for all eight universities who rejected Rob to admit Running Elk, that certainly goes well beyond random error.

It could be that the admissions people at each university, not looking at the social security numbers, noticed the two very similar applications and thought that Rob and Running Elk were identical twin brothers. This explains why they processed both applications, but it does not explain the decisions; randomness should not greatly favor one over the other.

Finally, could it be that the demand for places at these institutions changed between the time Rob and Running Elk applied? Perhaps Rob was rejected because when his application was received they thought there would be tons of them. When they did not materialize, the schools turned to Running Elk instead. After all, he is a pretty good substitute for Rob. This does not seem to be the answer either, because nationally this is the largest group of high school seniors on record, and there is no evidence of a drop off in demand during the short time period separating the applications of Rob and Running Elk. Besides, most of these places do batch admissions, evaluating all the applications together rather than as they come in, which gives no advantage or disadvantage to the later applicants.

The only plausible explanation is that Running Elk was admitted simply because, in this controlled experiment, he checked the box labeled "Native American." Like Groucho Marx, who would not join any club that would have him, I do not want to attend any university that admits me based on my ethnicity as opposed to my academic record. After all, isn't the point behind promoting diversity that we should not discriminate against people based on their ethnicity, their religion or their preferences? Then why should we discriminate in favor of people based on their ethnicity or anything else?

This fall I will be attending the University of Illinois. And shortly my name will legally once again be Robert Edward Taylor.

The reaction around school was immediate.

"Rob Taylor, you tell 'em!" Tim Tyler called loudly when he passed Rob in the hall.

"That's my boy, Rob, sticking it to The Man," Antoine Jackson said and laughed when he saw Rob in the cafeteria at lunchtime.

Only Norman "Nazi" Nelson seemed to be confused by it all.

Sarah caught up with Rob just outside of AP Euro.

"So it's Illinois, huh?" she asked with a grin. "Do we call you Rob again now?"

"Yes, Sarah, please call me Rob again. The name change should be legal in a couple of days," Rob said grinning back.

"What you did is very noble, turning down those places and the money, too. I'm really proud of you," she said softly.

"Thank you," he answered, a little embarrassed by Sarah calling him 'noble.' "How are you doing?"

"Not done yet, but I think I'm getting close. Although I still have to check on some details. And just like you, I have my own reasons for waiting to let it out. But I absolutely promise that I'll let you and Carrie know as soon as I make up my mind."

For the third time during the month of April, Sarah dropped in on Ms. Smith after school.

"I think I've almost decided, but I still have a few questions related to what happens after college."

"Let me see if I can answer them for you," Ms. Smith responded.

They had a far-reaching conversation for the next thirty minutes. There were some things Ms. Smith felt she could answer but others she was unsure about, so she suggested that Sarah ask those questions elsewhere.

"Also, there is a bit of a problem. It's the media. The local papers, the Chicago papers, Page at the *Sentinel*, the guy at AP, and even some of the radio stations and a few television stations have all been calling me wanting to interview me. I don't think I can do all these interviews."

"No problem," Ms. Smith responded, adjusting her glasses. "You know how they have national signing day for the high school athletes? It's really just a small press conference in most cases, but for top athletes they will have a full-scale event with lots of media. The person makes one announcement and takes all the questions at once. Talk to Mrs. K or someone in the principal's office about this. The school can easily set this up for you. They will send the information out and you can let all the people who've called you know about it."

"Do you want to know which way I'm leaning?"

"Actually I like a good surprise. I can wait," Ms. Smith said happily.

Sarah sent out a slew of e-mails once she got home. A number of them went to faculty members at Harvard whom Ben had put her in touch with. A few days later, after considering the responses, she told her parents what her decision was. They were quietly comfortable with it. She also called Ben, who was a little startled by her choice, and informed Kevin, who, being much younger, was oblivious to it.

That night Carrie and the newly renamed Rob came over. They brought cupcakes to celebrate, this time with a sparkler in each. She told them her choice.

"Congratulations," Carrie said beaming, glad that for Sarah it was finally over. Rob seemed rather surprised, given what he perceived her fondest wishes to be, but smiled broadly.

The next day, outside the main entrance to the high school, Rob had what started out as an unpleasant experience. A couple of sophomore football players, suffering from spring fever and hormonal problems, starting hassling him as he walked toward the building just before second period.

Because Rob was known as a "smart kid," one of them verbally abused him. When Rob responded in anger, the other, coming from a different angle, knocked his books down, called him a "geek," and then shoved him to the ground. They both towered over him.

Absorbed in their own deeds, they failed to notice Tim Tyler stepping out of a car ten feet away. Like Rob, he had ditched his first period class because he did not feel, as a senior in his last semester, that he should go that day. Tim covered the ten feet with the speed that only modern day athletes, especially if they are big men, possess. He blindsided the first sophomore, dropping his shoulder just as he reached him. Students sitting on the front lawn heard a sickening crunch as Tim drove him ten yards across the lawn into a row of bushes. When he turned, the observers swore that Tim resembled a Norse berserker, completely out of control, with bloodshot red eyes. He reached the other sophomore and lifted him like a bundle of sticks above his head, with the intention of throwing him out in the street.

"You don't ever touch a friend of mine!!" he screamed loud enough for everyone outside the main entrance to hear.

Six of Oak Stream's security guards, none of whom were small men, were on the scene at that point, having responded to the initial harassment when a supervisor radioed to them from in front of a monitor linked to the cameras outside the school. They eventually restrained Tim Tyler, but it took all of them several minutes to do so. During the struggle Tyler shouted at the sophomores, who looked on in a daze, telling them exactly which bones of theirs he was going to break when he caught up with them outside of school. His knowledge of anatomy was impressive.

Arthur Johnson, the dean of discipline at Oak Stream, met with Tim after the varsity football coach had a chance to calm him down. The three sat in Johnson's office, where the dean had spoken to Tim about his behavior on several previous occasions.

"Tim, I've seen the film from the security cameras, so I know what happened. I know you were trying to help, but I would appreciate it if you would let me do my job without intervening."

"Dean Johnson, I appreciate you asking me to do that. I'm sorry if I made your job harder," Tim said, in a bit of diplomacy that impressed even the football coach. "But that was my friend out there getting abused."

He paused and chose his words carefully.

"I would appreciate it, just so they don't misunderstand me, if you would tell those two sophomores that the only reason I'm letting this go is that you asked me to."

"Tim, I will let them know that I talked you into letting me handle it. I think they will be relieved that we'll be able to work this out through official channels. They'll both get suspended long enough to convince them of the error of their ways. And I know Coach Eck will impress upon them what proper behavior is for members of the football team. You're free to go back to class, Tim, and, off the record, I think Rob Taylor is lucky to have a friend like you." The dean was relieved that the incident had come to an end so easily.

The school scheduled the formal announcement by Sarah for Wednesday of the next week at 10:00 a.m. in the teachers' lounge on the third floor. It was a quiet day in the news world, so various members of the press were in the room, including Page Brooks from the *Sentinel*. She mingled with the veteran news people as if she was Johnny Deadline, Ace Reporter, telling all who would listen that she would be at Northwestern University next year. Mrs. K acted as a master of ceremonies in some sense, sitting at the front table with Sarah. Carrie, Rob, and a bunch of other seniors and friends of theirs had been excused from classes so that they could attend. Ms. Smith stood with them at the back of the room.

"I bet you it's Harvard," a blonde male reporter from the *Tribune* said to an attractive Latino woman who worked for the *Sun-Times*. He already had his story written and was waiting for Sarah to name the school so that he could insert it in the proper places. "Her brother goes there."

"What do you want to bet?"

"Five bucks."

"If you're so sure, you take Harvard, and I'll take the rest of the field."

The *Tribune* man thought a bit. "Then I'll need odds," he said.

"OK, how about five to one?"

"You're on," he said, sealing it with a handshake.

Mrs. K brought the session to order and introduced Sarah.

"It's been a long year," Sarah said with a sense of relief, "and the last month has probably been the hardest part of it. Having been admitted by so many fine universities made the decision especially difficult. I certainly appreciate that such a large number of schools saw fit to accept me when they have so many strong applicants. I also want to thank various people for the enormous amount of help they have given me. Ms. Smith from the history division and Mrs. K, my counselor, deserve special mention. As do my friends Carrie and Rob, who helped me when necessary and also made me do the things I had to do myself. Finally, there's my family. They suffered through this with me in various ways but also helped me more than they know."

"But, after all this, I've reached a decision. I'll be at Illinois next year."

There were a variety of puzzled expressions around the room, mostly from the press. Some of her classmates gasped when she said 'Illinois.' Ms. Smith, standing in the back, simply smiled. The guy from the *Tribune* took a fiver out of his pocket and glumly handed it to the woman from the rival paper. He would have to rewrite his story.

"Sarah, I'm sorry. Do you mean Northwestern University in Evanston?" a man with one of the Oak Stream community papers asked.

"No, I mean the University of Illinois in Urbana-Champaign."

"Why a state school when you've been accepted by almost all the finest private schools in the country?" someone in the back asked.

"There are several important factors in my decision," Sarah responded. "First, kids like me, who are not at the absolute top of the high school students in the country, can get a good education at any one of many different schools, especially because college is so much what you make of it. They have the necessary classes and, in my field, if I do exhaust the undergraduate offerings, I can take graduate courses during my senior year. Second, my family will give me a specific dollar amount each year toward my undergraduate education. If it costs more than that, I pay the rest. If it costs less than that, I keep the rest. Since I'm almost certainly going on to graduate school after this, I would rather conserve my resources for that than use them up when I'm an undergraduate. What I get from my parents will cover tuition plus room and board at Illinois and there will be some money left over, but it's nowhere near what it costs to go to a private school or a public school out of state. Honestly, the prospect of ending up $100,000 or more in debt to get an undergraduate degree in history frightens me a bit."

"But wouldn't you be better off going to a more prestigious undergraduate institution, in terms of what that name will do for you and how it will help you get into a good graduate school?" the *Sun-Times* reporter asked.

"I spoke with one of my teachers about that and checked around a bit myself. With a graduate degree, I'll be viewed based on the strength of that degree. Where you went to college is apparently largely ancient history once you have an advanced degree. No one pays much attention to it. Just like once you have a job, they don't worry about where you went to school. I've also heard that, in terms of getting into graduate school, what really matters is your undergraduate record and your standardized board scores, not so much where your degree is from. So attending a prestigious place apparently does not buy you a lot related to graduate school."

"Sarah, most people in your position would probably pick the most distinguished, or however you would describe it, undergraduate institution. Do you have any concerns that you might not be making the right decision?" Page Brooks asked.

"Beyond the logical arguments I just gave you, which I've thought long and hard about, I also looked at some evidence on this. In my own family, the people in my parents' and grandparents' generation largely chose colleges based on the financial aspects of the decision, meaning that they went to nearby state schools, because they were less expensive, or somewhere else because it was financially advantageous. They did just fine making the decision that way, and that was before everyone seemingly went to graduate school. Also, I looked at the careers of the Noble Prize winners in Economics. A number of them attended the nearest state school when they were undergraduates, and it didn't hurt them at all. So I have solid facts to back up my decision."[3]

Page Brooks seemed unhappy with the answer to her question.

"Are you saying that some of your fellow students at Oak Stream, who will be attending places like Harvard, Yale, and Stanford next year, made the wrong decision?" Page asked in an accusatory tone.

"No, not at all. In fact, a couple of people I'm close to are going to the University of Chicago, and I think it will be a really good place for them. Page, what I'm saying is that, broadly defined, there are no right versus wrong places to go to college. There are just different choices. If you were going to buy a car, is there only one kind of car that is right for everyone? Surely you wouldn't argue that everyone should buy the most expensive car or the least expensive car on the market. They will all get you around. It's a question of picking the one that works best for you, given your circumstances."

Page refused to give up. "So, according to you, an elite school is a waste."

Sarah gave Page a look that would have frozen her solid, even if she had been standing on the equator. "Page, are you writing a news story or an opinion piece for the *Sentinel*?" The veteran reporters in the audience laughed. "By the way, have you checked into exactly what happens at the 'elite' schools once you get there? At some you work really hard, because the classes are very demanding with term papers on top of the exams and the regular work. At others, it's more relaxed. Sure those schools are hard to get into, but if the curriculum is not very demanding, what's the value added in that? Is a university an educational experience or a finishing school?"

Recognizing that she was getting angry, Sarah stopped for a moment to settle herself.

"Look, I picked the school that's right for me, given my circumstances, and I'm quite happy with my decision. Page, I hope you checked carefully into the school you chose and that you're happy with it."

And Sarah was happy with her choice, even though it puzzled a lot of her extended family and neighbors.

---

[3] Malcolm Gladwell makes a somewhat similar point regarding the Nobel Laureates in Medicine and Chemistry in chapter 3 of his book *Outliers: The Story of Success*.

11
THE FINALE

A few days later, sensing that Carrie would like to talk, Sarah invited Carrie and Rob over to her house. Surprisingly, Rob arrived 15 minutes early, with a manila envelope in his hand.

"This is unlike you, Rob. You're early," she said in disbelief.

"I know. I wanted to ask you something," he responded.

"What?"

"Well . . ." he hemmed and hawed a bit. "Since we're seniors and we're going to the same place next year, I was wondering if you might like to go to the prom with me."

"Yes, Mr. Taylor, I would like to go to the prom with you. But you'll have to get dressed up. I won't go with you if you're in jeans and a T-shirt," Sarah said in jest.

"I know that. What color dress will you be wearing?"

"Green, almost certainly."

"How about if I wear this?" Rob asked, opening the envelope in his hand and paging through a catalog from a tuxedo chain. He pointed to a traditional charcoal grey tuxedo, right out of an early James Bond movie.

"Mr. Taylor, this looks very sophisticated," she said with a giggle, remembering Aunt Stephanie's summary remark about the desirable features of boys from outside the Midwest.

"I also thought, since we're going to prom and we'll both be at Illinois next year, maybe we could go to a movie or do some things together in the meantime?"

"Like go out on a date!? Damn, Rob, I've known you since second grade. I thought you'd never ask."

She moved toward him and kissed him on the cheek. Playfully, she took off his glasses.

"You know, if you got contact lenses I think you would look very cute."

He retrieved his glasses from her hand and for the time being put them back on his head.

Carrie arrived a few minutes later and seemed both happy and sad to learn their news.

"Would it be OK then if I just met you guys at prom and hung around with you? I know that makes me sort of a third wheel, but no one has asked me," Carrie said with a fair bit of remorse.

"Maybe no one has asked you yet, but someone has been asking about you," Rob interjected knowingly.

"Who? Tell me, Rob, or I will never speak to you again."

"Frank Foster. He asked me if you're going with anyone. I think he partly wanted to check whether I was going to ask you."

"Frank Foster? He's really smart," she gasped.

"Carrie, will you forget about academics for a minute!? He's really nice and he's good-looking," Sarah pleaded.

"Plus, you'll both apparently be at Chicago next year. He has notified them that he's going there in the fall. What do you want me to tell him?"

"Tell him I'm not going with anyone yet. Don't give anything away, but if he asks you, tell him that I would say 'yes' if he asks me. *Goddamn* it, Rob, use your very fertile imagination, but tell him whatever it takes to get him to ask me to prom!"

"I'll take care of it. And don't worry, I'll be discrete."

"Woo-hoo!" Carrie shouted, grabbing Sarah's hands and shaking them. "We're going to prom!"

"We'll have to coordinate the transportation and the other details, but Carrie and I can take care of that," Sarah said, suddenly becoming very 'female' regarding the minutiae of the event.

"Before you get carried away with ordering a limo or whatever, you should know that I've already picked out our ride for the evening. There's only room for two, though, so we'll have to meet Carrie and Frank there. Sorry about any problems that might cause, but we'll work it out."

Sarah wondered whether he had rented a horse or a bicycle for the evening.

"What did you get, Mr. Taylor?"

"It's a surprise. You have to wait until that night to find out."

"I see I've got a lot to tell my parents about," Carrie said, coming back to reality. "I have to figure out how I'm going to do this."

"You haven't told them yet about Chicago?" Rob asked.

"No, but there's no use waiting any longer. I'll tell them tomorrow night, assuming Frank asks me tomorrow."

After talking to Rob before school started, Frank asked Carrie to prom in the hall the next day. It was agreed that they would go as a foursome. The next evening Sarah waited in her room, with her cell phone at the ready, in case Carrie called or came over. Rob sensed that it was a night for girl talk and found somewhere else to be. He was right, because not long after 8 p.m. Carrie was at Sarah's bedroom door with an overnight bag. She looked rattled, like someone who had just been through combat.

"Carrie, what happened?"

"I thought I would tell my parents first that I was going to prom, thinking that because Frank is a valedictorian who's going to the University of Chicago it would not be a problem. I mean, really, how could anyone not like Frank Foster? Then my mother starts in with the usual negatives about 'You won't see him when you're at MIT,' having no idea how many people go to homecoming or prom with someone just to have fun. So I'm immediately defending myself because of prom. After a few minutes of her yelling, I tell her that I'm actually not going to MIT. Surprisingly, that shut her up for a bit, probably because it astonished the crap out of her. But when I told them that I was going to Chicago, it really hit the fan. My mother starts asking me whether this is Frank's idea and why am I letting this boy run my life and all this totally stupid stuff."

"Then what?"

"Then I told her that she's the one trying to run my life since I was born, not Frank, who had nothing to do with me going to Chicago. She then tells me that I'm ruining everything that she's worked for, that I'm an ingrate, and not to come back to her when my life is a mess."

"Then what happened?" Sarah asked apprehensively.

"I told her that this has been the problem since I was born. It's always her pushing for what she wants, not what I want, and maybe she should have asked me once or twice what it is that I want instead of being such a totally inconsiderate bitch."

"Then what?" Sarah shuddered at the thought of Carrie having this conversation with her mother.

"She called me a really bad name. I told her to go to hell, got my stuff, and came over here. Can I stay with you for a while?" Carrie begged.

"Sure, I'll get out a pillow and a sleeping bag, if you don't mind the floor."

"That's fine with me. I'll leave my father a message on his cell phone telling him where I am. I guess I made a mess of this, huh?" Carrie asked, instinctively expecting to be criticized.

"No you didn't, not at all. What was the alternative? Tell your mother first that you're going to Chicago and then tell her about prom? Do you think it would have been any different?"

"No, it wouldn't have been," she admitted with a shrug.

"Exactly. She would have gone off on you either way. Once you decided to go to Chicago, it was a done deal," Sarah assured her. "You're not the problem; she is. Just keep reminding yourself of that. Come on, Carrie, we'll start shopping for dresses this week. Prom's not that far off, you know. This will be a ton of fun."

The rest of the evening was strangely quiet as the girls watched television downstairs.

Rob heard the story at school the next day from Sarah, who begged him not to breathe a word to Frank Foster, lest he flee the scene. Rob agreed to keep quiet about it, although he told Carrie "Good for you" when she mentioned to him what she had said to her mother.

A cloud of uncertainty hung over Carrie's life until her father called her the next night while she was sitting with Rob and Sarah in the latter's bedroom after dinner. Her responses were brief and, to the listener, uninformative. When the conversation finished, she turned to her friends.

"As you can probably tell from my phone conversation, that was my dad. I'll be going back home tonight. Apparently he had a talk with my mother, meaning most likely that he screamed at her because that's the only way you can get her to listen, and she has accepted the idea of me going to prom and not going to MIT. They would like to meet Frank, which is a little problematic, since doesn't your prom date usually come over the night of prom?"

"No problem," Rob responded. "Since Sarah and I are officially dating, why don't the four of us go to a movie Saturday night? I can get my dad's car, pick up Sarah and Frank, and then come to your house. Frank can meet your parents with us there. The more people in the room, the harder it is to be unpleasant."

"Wow, that's a great idea. You guys would do this for me?"

"Of course we would. Remember, it's 'One for All and All for One.'"

Rob and Sarah picked up Frank at his sizable house in northwest Oak Stream on Saturday shortly before 6:30. They were both relieved that he was nicely dressed in khaki pants and a polo shirt with freshly polished dress shoes.

Mr. Wilson answered the door when they rang the bell at Carrie's much larger house.

"Sarah, Rob, come in. Hi, I'm Joe Wilson. You must be Frank," he said.

"Yes, Mr. Wilson, I'm Frank Foster," he responded, shaking Mr. Wilson's hand

Mrs. Wilson was polite but initially very distant. She and Mr. Wilson asked Frank the usual questions about himself and his family, probably the same ones they had answered when they had been teenagers meeting someone's parents for the first time.

"Where do you know Carrie from?" Mrs. Wilson inquired.

"We've been in class together for a few years."

"Did you go to Washington for middle school?"

"No, I was at Lincoln with Rob and Sarah."

"What does your father do?"

"He's a lawyer, Mrs. Wilson."

"Here in Oak Stream?"

"No, he's at one of the big firms downtown."

"Is your family from the Chicago area then?"

"No, not originally. My mother is from St. Louis. My father's family has been here since the 1830s. They came from Boston not long after the Erie Canal connected the Midwest to the East Coast."

"Both Mr. Wilson and I are from Massachusetts. My family came from England in the early 1700s," she said proudly. "When did your family come over?"

Carrie sensed that her mother was engaging in a very competitive game of one-upmanship regarding Frank's family tree.

"Actually, they came over a bit earlier than that. One of my Foster ancestors was on the ship after the *Mayflower*."

"All these years in history classes together and you never mentioned that, Frank?"

"It's not that big of a deal, Rob. It's kind of like having been at the dinner the night before the Last Supper."

It appeared, however, to be a big deal to Carrie's mother. She smiled frequently and was quite a bit nicer after that.

Carrie watched apprehensively as Sarah and Rob interjected little details and snippets of conversation here and there to make the encounter flow better. Carrie's mother asked questions of Rob and Sarah and seemed calmed by the fact that they were also dating. After a few minutes Mrs. Wilson excused herself to go upstairs, at which point the foursome pleaded that they needed to leave if they were going to be on time for the movie at the Lake Theater in downtown Oak Stream.

"Whew," Carrie exhaled as they walked down the front steps.

"That wasn't so bad, as far as meeting the parents goes," Frank offered innocently.

"Brother, you did good," Rob said without elaborating any further. He glanced over at Sarah.

"I bet my mother went upstairs to consult her early Massachusetts history books. By now she's probably checked the passenger list for the ship your ancestor came over on and has started constructing your family tree," Carrie said as she poked Frank in the ribs.

The evening went smoothly, even though Carrie and Frank had the usual awkwardness of two people on a first date. Rob and Sarah, having known each other for what seemed like most of their lives, were completely comfortable with one another. During the following weekends, the four of them went to museums and places downtown, including a quick swing through Hyde Park coupled with a visit to the massive Museum of Science and Industry, which they all remembered from grade school field trips.

As the prom approached, their schedule firmed up. They made plans to meet for dinner at a restaurant near the Loop and then go to the dance, which would be held at a downtown hotel. Frank's parents were hosting a post-prom party in their backyard for him and a number of his friends, which gave them a simple reason to say no to the various wild parties being held at summer homes in Wisconsin and Michigan. The Fosters were inviting adult friends of theirs and also the parents of the couples coming by after prom; however, they made it known that the alcohol was strictly for the adults.

The girls chose their dresses in the nick of time. Sarah's was a dark green, her signature color, toward the emerald end of the spectrum. Carrie picked something in a medium red, a color she favored given the tint of her hair and nails, which were polished for the first time and of decent, non-nervously-chewed length.

Rob was still mysterious about the transportation details, but told Sarah that he would come by at 5 p.m. for the usual pictures at a pre-prom event hosted by the Jennings. As she sat in the living room at the front of the house, adjusting her dress one more time, Sarah heard an engine purr in the street outside. Looking out, she saw a vintage 1960s silver gray Aston Martin DB5 pull up smoothly to the curb. Rob, without glasses and with his hair combed back a bit, hopped out and closed the door before stepping onto the parkway. When he reached the sidewalk, he adjusted both cuffs on his immaculate white shirt. Sarah, overcome by surprise, walked out to meet him rather than waiting for him to enter.

"*Dun . . . dun-dun . . . dun-dun-dun,*" Sarah hummed the theme from the James Bond movies as she approached. "Rob Taylor, where did you get this car?"

"It was supplied to me by Q, based on instructions from M," he said in return. "Do you like it?"

"Like it? It's the coolest car on earth. But how much did it cost?"

"Not that much. I didn't buy it; I rented it."

"But still," she gasped.

"You have to stop worrying about it, Sarah. Nothing is too good for you tonight."

Rob reached in the left side of his jacket with his right hand. Sarah wondered if he had a Walther PPK and was adjusting the shoulder holster. Instead, he pulled out a silver metal cigarette case and tilted it toward Sarah to offer her one.

"When did you start smoking?"

"Tonight," he said and grinned. "Actually I'm just offering them to others to be polite. Cigarettes cause cancer, you know."

"Yes, I heard something about that a while ago," she responded. "Are you going to be 'in character' all night?"

"Yes. Do you mind?"

"No, I think it's very *sophisticated*," she said with the broadest smile possible. "However, I'm imposing certain rules. Mr. Taylor, you are not to smoke any cigarettes this evening, and I refuse to call you James or double-oh-seven."

"Fair enough, Miss Jennings. But don't get too bossy or I'll . . ."

"Or you'll what?" She ran her finger down his nose playfully.

"Or I'll have to use the ejector seat when we're on the highway. The car has one on the passenger side, you know."

Sarah burst out laughing at the thought of her dress acting like a sail as she glided in the air above the Chicago metro area.

Their night, for several hours after that, was a whirlwind of activity with people flitting in and out of places. The one constant was the attention that they and the car received as they went from here to there. Sarah finally caught her breath at the prom itself. Rob, even though he disliked much of the current music, asked her to dance several times and was surprisingly proficient.

A number of people from Oak Stream, including Page Brooks and her friends, whom Sarah ran into in the ladies' room of the hotel, did not even recognize Rob.

"Sarah," Page asked excitedly after her friends went back to dance, "who is your date, and where did he get that car? Is he from New Baden or something? Does he have an older brother? Or even a younger brother? I'm just like here with a friend tonight, as opposed to dating this guy. So if he has a brother, I'd be really interested in meeting him."

Sarah laughed inside because none of these girls had paid Rob a second of attention during four years of high school. Especially Page, who actually had been dating her prom escort for several weeks.

At the end of the dance, the band's lead singer, a very attractive young woman, stepped up to the microphone. "Our final song for the evening is a request and it goes out to Sarah Jennings, from Rob Taylor. It's 'Dreaming' by Blondie."

Sitting at their table, Sarah looked at Rob with surprise. He simply held out his hands and motioned for her to dance. As they walked out, the floor filled up around them. They danced free form while the band pounded out the introduction, but when the singer took up the lyrics Rob took Sarah's hands in his and moved to a closed position. He led her through a series of turns and half-turns, leading with his left and then his right hand.

Next, Rob added a quarter turn and then turned underneath Sarah's arm. As he spun her around, the room and the people in it flashed by their eyes. Some of the crowd stopped and stared at them.

"Look at that boy go," Twan Jackson said to LaShawn Johnson.

"Man, has he got the moves."

"Damn right he does!"

Rob switched Sarah's hands so that his left held hers while her right was in his. They did a series of half turns in which first Sarah and then Rob turned.

At that point Rob introduced a couple of walk-bys in which he grabbed Sarah's hand and gave her a half turn after moving past her right side. Then he checked over his shoulder to make sure that there was room before dropping Sarah's hands and taking several steps backward to return to free form. The circle of people around them, clapping to the beat, widened to give him room.

Rob windmilled back toward Sarah and took her hands in his again. She flew clockwise and counterclockwise during the last stanza of the song as he combined the best of the moves they had done so far.

"Whew!" Sarah exclaimed when they came to a stop. "I've never danced like that before. I feel like I'm in a dream."

"May your dreams always come true."

"They have," Sarah replied. She paused for a moment.

"Rob, no offense meant, but I don't remember you being such a good dancer."

"Well, since we were going to prom and there was a band, I figured I better learn. My mother is actually a very good dancer. She even taught my father, if you can believe that. So I asked her to show me how to dance to this type of song. We've been practicing ever since I asked you to prom. It's really pretty simple. Those are just the basic steps from swing dancing, except now the beat is a four count instead of a six count."

"And the song? Where did that come from? Somehow I don't think that it's a standard for most bands today."

"I contacted them and, for a price, they learned it and agreed to make it the last song. I thought they did a good job."

"Oh, yes, they did," she said firmly."

The post-prom party at the Fosters's was a great capstone to a beautiful evening. They arrived when it was already crowded because Rob insisted on taking Sarah for a spin down Lake Shore Drive after the dance. Carrie was standing in the middle of the floodlight-illuminated yard, with her hand in Frank's, a semicircle of people around them. She smiled brightly as Rob and Sarah walked up.

"Rob, the girls have been staring at you all night. And that was before you cut loose on the dance floor," blurted out Joey Merlino, who was the fashion plate in their class. Kathy Bates, his date, nodded in agreement. She had blossomed into one of the prettiest girls at Oak Stream. She also bloomed academically, really buckling down after her sophomore year. As a result, she had had two papers accepted by *Interpretations* her senior year, as many as Carrie, Sarah, and Rob and one more than Frank Foster and Joey Merlino.

"Sorry, but Rob is unavailable," Sarah said happily as she squeezed his arm.

"Where will you guys be next year?" Rob asked.

"Kathy and I are both going to Illinois," Joey responded.

"Then we'll be seeing each other around."

"It's a long time since honors history our freshman year guys," Frank remarked philosophically, looking at the composition of the group.

"Some of you guys have changed quite a bit," Rob observed. "I remember what a bunch of nerds you were back then."

"What's that phrase? About the pot calling the kettle black?"

The people near them broke out laughing as Joey Merlino pretended to strangle Rob.

"Seriously," Frank continued, "isn't it funny–did I just say an oxymoron?–how things turn out? Remember after homecoming junior year, when we were sitting in the park talking about what we were going to do in the future? We were all going to Harvard, Stanford, Oxford, and places like that, as far away from Oak Stream as possible."

"Except for you, Joe. Weren't you going to wander the world for a few years in search of adventure? Visit Tibet and Nepal? Walk the entire length of the Great Wall of China? Find some lost pyramids in Egypt and recover their treasures?" Carrie asked.

"Actually, that's on hold for a while until I finish my accounting degree." He laughed when he said it, realizing that the business world had few openings for wandering global accountants.

"Look how we ended up," Frank stated. "None of us are leaving the state of Illinois."

They turned as a tremendous stomping sound, made by someone approaching from the direction of the bar, came from behind them.

"Taylor! Dude, you look great. Never knew you had it in you," Tim Tyler screamed as he walked up to the group. "You absolutely have to let me drive that car!"

"Tim, buddy, first of all you won't fit in it. Second of all, it starts to shake if you go over one-fifty. Third of all, I have to return it in immaculate condition tomorrow morning or they will claim my firstborn. So, unfortunately, I have to say no."

Tyler picked Rob up and gave him a bear hug just as Antoine Jackson came over with his date. Antoine was in a light green tux and wore green alligator shoes. He eyed Tyler wearily, setting his drink on a table with his left hand and gently moving his date to one side with his right and then stepping forward after he had cleared the decks for action. The entire group tensed.

"You had better goddamn well put him down." The words marched like a parade of giants out of Antoine's mouth. "Or, party or no party, you and I are going to have a serious problem."

"Twan, it's all good," Rob said, clarifying the situation from midair.

Tim Tyler eased Rob down next to Sarah.

"You two are cool?" Jackson asked in return.

"We are *very* cool, Mr. Jackson," Tim added. "This is my best pal."

"Actually, he's *my* best pal," said Twan.

"OK, I'm willing to share him with you. Would you like access to Rob alternate months or weeks?"

"Every other day would be fine—if you won't be needing him."

"Not at all. You may have him whenever you wish."

Tim bowed and moved his hand down and toward Antoine in a flourish straight out of the seventeenth century.

"Excellent. Thank you, sir," Antoine said as he bowed in return.

The tension in the crowd drained as quickly as it had mounted, and everyone burst out laughing at the banter.

"Twan, I heard you decided to go to Illinois," Rob said.

"Yes, you talked me into it, helped me apply, and they accepted me. Since they were nice enough to let me in, the least I can do is attend."

"You'll do fine there."

"Mr. Tyler, I understand you'll be there next year playing football," Antoine continued.

"Yup, I'm looking forward to it."

"You should meet my friend Clark Walker when you get there. I'll introduce you."

"The wide receiver?! He's awesome! If he stays healthy he has a legitimate shot at not just making a team in the NFL but at a long professional career."

"He's one of my boys from the West Side. You can get to know the guys on the football team through him, and he'll introduce you to some of the basketball players too."

"I'll be glad to meet them. Thanks for that."

"No problem. I guess I'll be seeing you around at Illinois then."

"You can count on it."

Tim and Antoine smiled at each other and shook hands.

"Sarah, would you like something to drink?" Rob asked solicitously.

"Yes, please. I'll have a diet Coke," she said, turning toward him as he started in the direction of the bar.

Rob stood in line a few minutes, taking out his cigarette case just as the couple in front of him received their drinks. He extended it to the forty-something male bartender who was a veteran of innumerable clubs and parties.

"Not while I'm on duty, but thanks anyway."

"I'll have a Vesper martini and a diet Coke."

"What kind of martini?" asked the bartender, not sure what he'd heard.

Rob named the ingredients and their measures.

"Like in the James Bond movies?" The bartender had seen many affected young men and women before, but Rob carried it off so well that he could not even think of laughing.

"Yes."

"Shaken, not stirred?"

"Absolutely. It bruises the gin." Rob paused before continuing. "Hey, I'm just kidding you about the martini. How about a regular Coke and a diet Coke?"

The bartender laughed and gave him two soft drinks. Rob returned to the circle of people he'd left a few minutes ago. The group that had been thrown together in Mr. Harrison's class during their freshman year, never imagining that they would become close friends, sipped their drinks and bantered for another hour.

As the party was winding down, Rob drove Sarah home just before her curfew. They quietly walked to the front door.

"Rob, this was just perfect. I had a wonderful time," she said with a full-moon-sized smile.

"So did I."

They put their arms around each other and kissed for several minutes, which seemed like several hours in the years following when they recalled this moment in their minds.

"Not much of senior year left now," Rob observed.

"In some ways, Rob, I'll say amen to that. But we still have graduation and the fun that goes along with it."

The graduation ceremony in the football stadium, on a warm but not hot June day, came off without a hitch. From their chairs Carrie, Rob, and Sarah could see Frank on the stage with the valedictorians. He looked for them in the sea of caps and gowns, smiling as he made eye contact. In his speech Frank mentioned the friendships formed in high school as his most important memories. He also touched on how what was behind them connected to what lay ahead.

Sarah's graduation party, in her backyard, was that weekend and most of the relatives and neighbors who had been at Ben's two years ago were there. As she talked to Carrie (Frank was detained at a family event), Rob brought over three small glasses of white wine.

"Sarah, give us a toast," he suggested, handing her a Chardonnay.

"For the three of us? After everything we've been through since freshman year? There's only one thing it could be. 'One for All and All for One.' I think that sums up our four years together perfectly."

There was a tear in her eye. They raised their glasses and clinked them lightly together.

"I have graduation gifts for you guys," Sarah said.

"And we have gifts for you, too," Rob responded.

From their size and shape, five of the six presents were clearly books. Predictably, they were history books. The last present, which Sarah gave to Rob, was longer and flatter than a book. He peeled off the wrapping paper to find a cream-colored wooden board with green letters on it.

"I made it in art class. You can hang it in your dorm room next year. Or I'll come over and hang it for you. Among other things, it pretty much describes this past year or so for me."

It read: "A man travels the world over in search of what he needs and returns home to find it." George Moore (1873-1958).

She leaned over and kissed him on the cheek.

At the other end of the yard, her brother Kevin was surrounded by a circle of adult relatives. Short for his age, he resembled an 1880s downtown building dwarfed by modern skyscrapers.

"Kevin, honey," Grandma Mary said, "you know it's never too early to start thinking about college. There are many fine Catholic universities out there to choose from."

"Mom . . ." her uncle Joe interrupted loudly, beginning his own sermon about the infinite value of an Ivy League education.

Looking across the yard at her brother, Sarah thought that she saw Kevin's head start to spin.

ABOUT THE AUTHOR

John Binder's children all graduated from Oak Stream High School, where they took classes from Ms. Smith.

He can be contacted at wsidejack@yahoo.com

Additional Resources:

Book website: www.girlwhoappliedeverywhere.com

14697906R00092

Made in the USA
Charleston, SC
26 September 2012